NAUGHTY NOUNS IN HISTORICAL ROMANCE

SYNONYMS TO SPICE UP YOUR STEAMY SCENES

THESAURUS FOR ROMANCE WRITERS

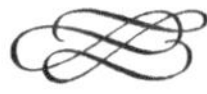

LIZ ADAMS

NAUGHTY NOUNS IN HISTORICAL ROMANCE
SYNONYMS TO SPICE UP YOUR STEAMY SCENES
THESAURUS FOR ROMANCE WRITERS

Published by: Writer's Fun Zone Publishing

ISBN-13: 978-1-944841-69-0

CONTENTS

PART 2: BARROOM, BEDROOM, AND PILLOW TALK

PRAISE FOR LIZ ADAMS' FICTION

5 stars! Oh my, Alice!

"Alice in Wonderland is truly a one of a kind book to begin with, but to be able to completely rewrite it in a very adult fashion takes talent. The author sticks true to characters Alice meets in the original books but now all encounters are very sexual in nature. Love [Alice's Salacious Adventures: Lessons From Wonderland]! Can't wait to read the next book!"

—Nic & Kenzie C.

5 stars! This book has everything

"I really enjoyed [Alice's Story of O: The Princess and the Pea]. It was so well written and it is very good. I will definitely read this book over again and recommend it!!"

—Carol Albertson-Breckenridge

5 stars! Dived in

"First time reading [Liz Adams], and wow I was sucked in. Loved [de Sade & Grimm: A Steamy Collection of Dark Delights] and I want more. I highly recommend."

—munchkinbetty

5 stars! Liz Adams does it again

"[Sherlock: The Casebook of a Salacious Sleuth] is a book with four spicy stories all relating to Sherlock Holmes. They are fun and steamy and the cases are interesting in each. If you love erotica, Liz Adams is definitely someone you should be reading."

—Taryn Schilling

INTRODUCTION TO THE THESAURUS SERIES

This is a thesaurus series I wish I had when I started writing sex scenes. While writing about a coupling, I'd spend countless hours searching for synonyms. When I wrote spicy historical scenes, I spent even more time working out if the synonyms were relevant to the time period I was writing in.

I wrote this thesaurus series for myself where here, in one trilogy of books, I can find powerful verbs and adjectives to improve my writing, plus plenty of historically accurate nouns to give my stories a flavor of authenticity.

OVERVIEW OF HOW THIS SERIES IS ORGANIZED

This thesaurus series is divided into three main sections: verbs, adjectives, and historical nouns. One book for each.

Voluptuous Verbs: The verbs are organized from early stages of desire to recovery from a sweaty bout of amorous aerobics.

Arousing Adjectives: The adjectives are organized from describing the body from head to toe, and all of the excitement that happens along the journey.

Naughty Nouns (This book): The nouns are organized by date of first popular use from head to toe, then to genitals; then from foreplay to the full snog.

A NOTE ABOUT LANGUAGE

At first glance, many of the verbs and adjectives may seem odd or misplaced. That's where your creativity comes in. For example, instead of, "She accommodated his entrance," you could write, "She negotiated his entrance." In context, the reader would understand the sentence.

A NOTE ABOUT HOW THE BOOKS ARE FORMATTED

I've formatted the print edition and the digital edition a little differently due to the benefit of each format.

If you have the print version of this book, I've left space beside the words in case you want to jot down your thoughts on a particular word, i.e., which ones would be great for explicit scenes, which would be great for subtle scenes, which would be great for the meet cute, etc. You can also note your favorite words in the "Personal Favorites" section at the end of the book.

If you have the digital version, you may be able to underline or highlight your favorite terms. Optionally, others with the ebook version might see which terms you (anonymously) underlined, and you might see the terms they underlined. So that can give you real-time feedback on the words all users of this ebook like the most.

A NOTE ABOUT LANGUAGE - TRIGGER WARNING

WARNING: Many of the words are profane, and some are even insulting and violent. Don't read this book if profanity and violent terminology offends you. You have been warned!

Happy word hunting!

BUT WAIT! THERE'S MORE! - BONUS PRINTABLE WORKSHEET

Go to LizAdamsAuthor.com/thesaurus to download a handsome worksheet you can use to keep notes of your favorite verbs, adjectives, and historically accurate nouns.

WHO THIS THESAURUS SERIES IS FOR AND NOT FOR

WHO THIS SERIES IS FOR

The *Thesaurus for Romance Writers* series is not just for romance authors. The trilogy is for any writer who has a sex scene in their story and wants to be sure the quality of the scene matches the experience the writer is trying to convey.

If you want to convey a subtle, intimate connection between the characters, this book can help you find the language you need. Want to make the reader experience an insatiable lust that requires hands-on reading? This thesaurus has just the words you're looking for.

Genres can include anything from spicy romance, to paranormal tales, to thrillers, to sci-fi adventures, as long as there is at least one scene of sexual intimacy.

WHO THIS SERIES IS NOT FOR

This thesaurus is not for writers of sweet romance nor any genre that doesn't include any sex scenes. Also, profanity and naughty words coat the pages, including words that can sound aggressive and negative. If such language may upset you, this is not the book for you.

MORE THAN JUST A NOUNS THESAURUS

How would you like to learn how to spice up your sex scenes beyond beefing up your nouns?

At the end of this *Naughty Nouns* thesaurus, I've added several appendices.

- Appendix A: Historical Sex Scene Planner *(Plan your scene by making decisions on the historical setting, clothing, and circumstances)*
- Appendix B: A Tip, Just the Tip - Using Historical Synonyms *(Incorporate historical nouns while keeping the scene arousing)*
- Appendix C: Find and Replace *(Make the prose sound historical without using archaic words)*
- Appendix D: Liz's Favorites — Nouns *(Be inspired by my favorite nouns from this thesaurus)*

These additions to the thesaurus contain a sampling of my writing method. Have fun with them!

NAUGHTY NOUNS: HOW TO USE THIS BOOK

Designed for authors of historical fiction, this thesaurus of naughty nouns aims to help you write scintillating sex scenes. I recommend you flip through the book and explore what works for you. Come up with your own way of interacting with this thesaurus!

Because roadmaps are useful, here's a suggested approach on how to use this book:

1. Before you write each sex scene, first answer the questions in "Appendix A: Historical Sex Scene Planner Template."
2. Next, finish the first draft of your entire novel and edit it, getting the story to a polished state for publication, before addressing the grammar and spelling.
3. For ideas to improve your sex scenes, read "Appendix B: A Tip, Just the Tip - Using Historical Synonyms."

4. Choose one sex scene within your novel to edit.
5. **Prose** - Open to Part 1, the "Useful Historical Prose" section of this book. Review the nouns in your sex scene, and confirm whether your choice of suggestive and explicit nouns in your prose fit the historical time period of your story. If they don't, adjust the words to what you think would sound better and fit the period. The chapters within the "Useful Historical Prose" section are ordered from head to toe, then the sexual experience from start to finish. As a bonus, historical verbs are added at the end of this book. As you change your drafted nouns to stronger, more specific nouns, be sure to note down the nouns you like in the "Personal Favorites" section of the paperback, or underline them in the ebook version.
6. **Dialogue** - Open to Part 2, the "Barroom, Bedroom, and Pillow Talk" section of the book and decide how polite or how vulgar each character is. Then insert the nouns that match their personality, making sure the words match the period. This section is also ordered from head to toe, followed by the chronological order of the sexual experience.
7. Lastly, go to "Appendix C: Find and Replace" and follow the instructions to make the text sound more historical. The appendix is more of a guide than a concrete set of laws. Use what works for you. The "Find and Replace" appendix is what I use to make my own scenes sound historical.

If this process is tiring and takes the fun out of your writing, do not use this process! If you don't have fun writing the scenes, your readers won't have fun reading them. Remember, find a process that works best for you.

INTRODUCTION TO HISTORICAL NOUNS

Ah, nouns. I never grow weary of using nouns.

Neither has anyone else in the entire existence of the written word. Even hieroglyphics had nouns. Which obviously begs the question, what would an ancient Egyptian version of *Fifty Shades of Grey* look like in hieroglyphics?

Fortunately, our English language has multiple words for all sorts of saucy unmentionables. This thesaurus provides an abundance of such synonyms.

Let's address some common questions.

WHAT ARE NOUNS?

A noun is a person (Wolverine), place (sauna), or thing (ramrod), sounding very much like an answer to a Clue game (Colonel Mustard in the library with a knife). Nouns include pronouns (she, he, they, it).

The world is a much better place with nouns because, let's be honest, a sentence without a noun is like a ____ without a ____.

HOW CAN I MENTION GENITALIA IN AN AROUSING WAY WITHOUT SOUNDING LIKE A DOCTOR LECTURING ON BODY PARTS?

Wow! What a great question! So great, in fact, that in "Appendix B: A Tip, Just the Tip," I address the challenge of describing naughty bits in a tantalizing way.

In a nutshell, it's best to replace the clinical words for genitalia with suggestive, emotional words while avoiding laughable euphemisms.

HOW IS NAUGHTY NOUNS ORGANIZED?

There are two main sections to this book: "Useful Historical Prose," which are nouns useful for historical prose, and "Barroom, Bedroom, and Pillow Talk," a list of nouns that can be used for bawdy dialogue.

In each of these two main sections, the chapters are ordered from head to toe, then focus on common erogenous zones, sexual acts, and lastly, the hot liquids of pleasure.

To find your synonyms, consider the historical period you're writing and check that the nouns you're using have entered the language.

For example, if you are writing a sex scene that takes place in the 1600s, you can make sure your choice of nouns are ones that were used in or before the 1600s.

In this book, there are additionally some verbs organized by date. Bonus!

SHOULD I USE OLD SYNTAX WITH OLD NOUNS?

If you're writing a sex scene that takes place in a different historical period, it's a good idea to have your terms match as closely as you can to the terms used in that period. The point isn't to make the writing authentic for a specific historical period. That would be too challenging for the reader to comprehend. Plus, it would yank them out of the story. I would venture a guess that most readers are not looking to read stories in the style of Chaucer. Most readers can't read old English.

Instead, your job is to add the flavor of the historical environment to wet the reader's tastebuds. Or nether regions. You can do that by sprinkling in an evocative "old" noun, all the while maintaining modern spelling and syntax. So your book will be readable to a modern audience and evocative of the historical setting.

In other words, it's better to write, "You soon shall be tasked with further duties," than "Thine tasks hither come anon."

IS THERE A WAY TO USE OLD-SOUNDING SYNTAX WITHOUT CONFUSING THE READER?

Syntax is the order of the words in a sentence, a handy tool when you want to write about a historical period without sounding like Chaucer, as I described in the previous section.

More important than the choice of words, I've found the placement and conjugation of the verb to be a better way of adding the flavor of historical fiction.

For example, instead of writing, "He ate a yummy salad often," you can write it as, "Often did he eat a salad worthy of kings." Notice that frequency, words like "often" and "always" and "never," work better at the start of a sentence to sound archaic. But, as I mentioned earlier, archaic-sounding syntax can cause the reader to struggle with comprehending the words, so the syntax may pull them out of the story. Use sparingly, is my advice.

Whatever you choose to do, be it using old-sounding

phrasing or keeping the syntax modern, choose your favorite synonym to evoke your story's historical period.

A NOTE ON SYNONYM SOURCES

To give credit where credit is due, most of the words in this thesaurus come from Jonathon Green's online interactive timeline of slang. The words were extracted from British books, including Chaucer and Shakespeare. It's quite possible the words first entered the English language earlier than written, so this is a guide to the earliest known record of the words.

As a result, my attribution of what period the words were used may be off. Nonetheless, these dated words are a great way to drizzle historical flavor throughout your manuscript.

A WORD ON GENDER LANGUAGE

When I describe a relationship in this book, for the purposes of clarity and convenience, the protagonist is female, and the protagonist's partner is male. These descriptions can be applied to LGBTQ+ scenes by changing the pronouns.

Enjoy!

PART 1: USEFUL HISTORICAL PROSE

LOVER

TRUE LOVE

1100s:

1175 Dear

1200s:

1200 Spouse

1206 Husband/Wife

1225 Lover

1300s:

1300 Loved one

1398 Beloved

1500s:

1503 Paramour

1573 Mate

1576 Sweetheart/Sweetie
1596 Darling

1700s:
1749 Partner

1800s:
1822 Boyfriend/Girlfriend
1839 Baby

1900s:
1906 Honey/Hon
1942 Pumpkin
1969 Dom(me)/Sub
1970 Master/Slave (a consenting relationship)

SNOG PARTNER

1500s:
1550 Companion

1900s:
1970 Fuck buddy
1995 Friend with benefits

OBJECTIFICATION

1300s:
1300 Conquerer/Conquest
1300 Master/Slave (without consent)

1375 Slut

1500s:
1500 Victim
1530 Breeder
1530 Whore

1700s:
1750 Instrument
1750 Assailant of choice

2000s:
2005 Cum bucket
2005 Cum dumpster

EYES

1500s:
  1561 Peepers

1600s:
  1654 Twinklers

1700s:
  1747 Peeps

1800s:
  1860 Windows (to her soul)

MOUTH, LIPS, AND TEETH

1300s:
- 1367 Maw

1500s:
- 1577 Chops

1700s:
- 1722 Gab
- 1776 Trap

1800s:
- 1880 Yawp

1900s:
- 1902 Feeder
- 1908 Jib

LIPS

1500s:

- 1577 Chops
- 1590 Chaps

TEETH

1500s:

- 1598 Grinders

1700s:

- 1739 Fangs
- 1796 Ivories

1900s:

- 1915 Pearly whites
- 1950 Chompers

STOMACH

1800s:

- 1821 Middle
- 1848 Tum
- 1850 Tummy

1900s:

- 1969 Love handles
- 1998 Six-pack

2000s:

- 2000 Eight-pack

HANDS, FISTS, AND FEET

HANDS

1500s:
- 1551 Claws
- 1593 Paws

1800s:
- 1800 Gropers
- 1812 Mittens
- 1827 Graplers
- 1844 Feelers
- 1859 Dukes
- 1859 Grabbers
- 1893 Mitts

1900s:
- 1911 Hams
- 1911 Meat hooks

1969 Clams

FISTS

1800s:
- 1812 Mittens
- 1885 Dukes

1900s:
- 1981 Guns

FEET

1500s:
- 1597 Hoofs

1800s:
- 1848 Tootsies

BREASTS

1200s:

- 1200 Bosom

1500s:

- 1507 Paps

1600s:

- 1654 Globes
- 1674 Heavers
- 1681 Boobies

1700s:

- 1708 Udders
- 1788 Titties

1800s:

- 1826 Boobs
- 1862 Tits
- 1888 Pair
- 1890 Knockers

1900s:

- 1939 Rack
- 1952 Hooters
- 1957 Jugs
- 1959 Cans
- 1963 Puppies

MALE GENITALS

PARTS OF THE PENIS (TOP TO BOTTOM)

Head
- Tip
- Tiny slit
- Prepuce (foreskin)
- Shaft
- Base
- Roots
- Sack
- Testicles

FULL GENITALS

1400s:
- 1465 Jewels

1500s:
- 1546 Giblets

1700s:
- 1707 Charms

1900s:
- 1966 Crown jewels
- 1969 Nards
- 1972 Package
- 1997 Junk

PENIS

1400s:

- 1460 Pin
- 1499 Lance

1500s:

- 1500 Cod
- 1500 Instrument
- 1533 Iron
- 1540 Tool
- 1540 Yard
- 1560 Prick
- 1573 Pike
- 1580 Manhood
- 1590 Weapon
- 1591 Rod

1600s:

- 1607 Pole

1619 Cock
1620 Quill
1625 Column
1653 Spigot
1653 Staff

1700s:
1700 Truncheon
1750 Throbbing mass
1768 Ramrod
1772 Shaft
1780 Gland

1800s:
1816 Poker
1836 Dick
1843 Rod
1863 Johnson
1865 Schlong
1890 Doodle
1890 Member

1900s:
1934 Whang
1935 Wiener
1947 Length
1948 Wong
1966 Thingy
1971 Unit
1987 Boner

TESTICLES

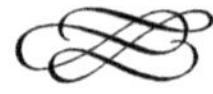

1300s:

1366 Ballocks

1400s:

1460 Ballock-stones

1460 Stones

1466 Eggs

1500s:

1508 Balls

1566 Cods

1600s:

1696 Pair

1800s:

- 1837 Nuts
- 1879 Bollox
- 1888 Ball bag
- 1889 Sack

1900s:

- 1918 Glands
- 1932 Cojones
- 1948 Rocks
- 1964 Nads
- 1971 Nutsack
- 1973 Jewels

2000s:

- 2001 Satchel
- 2003 Bollock bag
- 2008 Nut bag

ERECT PENIS

1500s:

- 1589 Come aloft
- 1597 Standing

1600s:

- 1606 Stalk
- 1653 Stiff and stout
- 1680 Cocked

1800s:

- 1840 Baton
- 1842 Spike
- 1864 Hard-on
- 1888 Stiff (having a bit of stiff)
- 1890 Bayonet
- 1893 Hard-on

1900s:

- 1935 Get it up
- 1944 Woodie
- 1958 Boner
- 1968 Stiffy
- 1992 Sprung
- 1993 Wood
- 1993 Morning wood
- 1998 Stiffer

2000s:

- 2005 Truncheon

LARGE PENIS

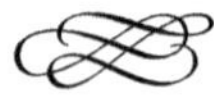

1600s:

- 1620 Hung
- 1682 Lobcock

1700s:

- 1748 Stretcher

1800s:

- 1979 Tosser

1900s:

- 1928 Hose
- 1963 Whopper
- 1972 Dangler
- 1972 Stacked
- 1994 Packing

VAGINA

1300s:

- 1325 Cunt
- 1386 Quaint
- 1386 Quoniam

1400s:

- 1495 Lap
- 1495 Trench

1500s:

- 1550 Quiver
- 1580 Sheath
- 1584 Altar of Venus
- 1590 Lips
- 1591 Venus's cradle
- 1594 Ring
- 1599 Cunny

1600s:

1600 Nest
1600 Nonny
1600 Rose
1600 Womb
1602 Muff
1604 Gap
1609 Orchard
1611 Notch
1612 Furrow
1620 Garden
1640 Slit
1650 Vitals
1656 Nether lips
1656 Twat
1656 Cauldron
1660 Orifice
1673 Alcove
1680 Altar
1680 Cloven spot
1683 Entrance
1690 Crack

1700s:

1700 Sluice
1705 Forge
1705 Quim
1707 Garden of Venus
1719 Kitty
1732 Sex
1748 Cleft
1775 Shrine of Venus
1785 Snatch

1786 Charms
1786 Gash
1797 Grove of Venus

1800s:
1801 Temple of Venus
1808 Merry bit
1826 Gulf of Venus
1833 Tunnel
1834 Belly
1836 Crevice
1837 Down below
1840 Quint
1843 Clam
1879 Pussy
1879 Quimmy
1888 Coo
1888 Front entrance
1888 Moistened aperture
1888 Motte
1890 Downy bit
1890 Garden of Eden
1891 Cave
1892 Chasm
1892 Heaven

1900s:
1900 Pussycat
1902 Naughty
1904 Vestry
1927 Beaver
1927 Bit of tail

1935 Minge
1966 Cooch
1966 Slash
1969 Muffin
1972 Nookie
1983 Maw
1985 Package
1995 Kitten

FEMALE GENITALS

CLIT

1600s:
- 1600 Nub
- 1680 Clit
- 1680 Clitoris

1900s:
- 1966 Dot
- 1999 Love button

2000s:
- 2007 Pearl

LABIA

1600s:
- 1604 Nonny-nonny

1630 Folds

1800s:

1888 Cunt lips

1900s:

1990 Labes

PUBIC HAIR

1500s:

1525 Beard
1593 Fur

1600s:

1600 Bush
1638 Moss
1659 Thicket
1660 Tuft
1665 Muff

1700s:

1772 Stubble
1797 Brush

1800s:

1833 Thatch
1844 Hair
1864 Shrubs

1875 Fluff
1880 Fuzz
1883 Plush
1888 Fleece
1888 Pussy
1890 Down

1900s:
1927 Beaver
1939 Rug
1939 Whiskers
1942 Mop
1953 Cunt hair
1960 Pussy hair
1966 Garden
1966 Lawn
1969 Trim
1982 Velvet

2000s:
2000 Hedge
2006 Minge

THE ACT OF CUNNILINGUS

1700s:

1744 A larking

1800s:

1888 A cunt-licking
1888 An eating
1895 A face job
1898 A sucking

1900s:

1927 A tongue lap
1928 Going downtown
1934 Getting down on it
1934 Sucking off
1939 Eating pussy
1941 Go down south
1943 Muffing
1946 Chewing

1963 Lap it up
1964 Sitting on his face
1965 A licking out
1965 A scarfing
1965 A tongue job
1967 A fressing
1969 Eating her out
1971 A muff job
1971 A pussy eating
1972 A lick

2000s:

2000 A muff munching

THE ACT OF FELLATIO

1700s:

1744 A larking

1800s:

1873 A mouth fuck

1879 A cocksucking

1879 A minetting

1900s:

1905 A suck off

1927 A tongue-lapping

1929 A sucking

1940 A cocksuck

1941 A suck

1946 A blow

1948 A blow job

1949 A b.j.

1954 A gam

1965 A hum job
1965 A prick-sucking
1965 A tongue job
1970 A job
1971 A hummer
1972 A mouth job
1973 Deep throat
1989 A knobber
1992 Lip action

2000s:

2002 A face-fucking
2003 A suck job
2011 A slurp

ASS

1300s:

- 1363 Bum
- 1376 Arse

1500s:

- 1533 Backside
- 1568 Behind
- 1576 Buttocks

1600s:

- 1607 Cheeks
- 1650 Hillocks

1700s:

- 1761 Ass
- 1768 Rear
- 1774 Derrière

1777 Posterior
1794 Bottom

1900s:
1923 Heinie
1926 Booty
1951 Buns
1958 Tush
1984 Glutes
1990 Bum crack
1993 Back
1993 Tushy
1994 Can
1997 Butt crack

RECTUM

1400s:

1400 Arsehole

1500s:

1533 Nock

1535 Channel

1592 Backdoor

1594 Anus

1600s:

1681 Bum

1682 Back gate

1700s:

1725 Rectum

1790 Crevice

1800s:

- 1838 Crack
- 1865 Asshole
- 1866 Bumhole
- 1888 Back entrance
- 1890 Ring

1900s:

- 1927 Flue
- 1930 Keister
- 1934 Alley
- 1934 Tail
- 1942 Butthole
- 1945 Back
- 1972 Alleyway

2000s:

- 2011 Back alley

ANAL SEX

1500s:

- 1598 Bardash

1600s:

- 1675 Fuck

1800s:

- 1800 Buried in her entrails
- 1874 Up her bowels
- 1879 Bumfuck
- 1879 Stuff

1900s:

- 1925 Take it up the ass
- 1950 Prat
- 1950 Seat
- 1962 Pack

- 1965 Buttbang
- 1965 Buttfuck
- 1970 Bum
- 1971 Saddle
- 1980 Rump
- 1980 Shoot in the tail
- 1984 Backdoor
- 1994 Bone

2000s:

- 2001 Caboose
- 2003 Split the peach
- 2004 Bust her ass

DESCRIPTION OF INTERCOURSE – GERUNDS

1300s:

1380 Swiving

1500s:

1520 Clipping
1560 Pleasuring
1568 Fucking
1593 Stroking
1598 Grinding

1600s:

1608 Niggling
1619 Clicketing
1633 Doing
1654 Knocking
1660 Frigging

1700s:
- 1705 Shoving
- 1705 Stitching
- 1707 Poking
- 1712 Jerking
- 1725 Nobbing
- 1738 Stuffing
- 1788 Mowing
- 1788 Shagging

1800s:
- 1811 Relishing
- 1834 Trouncing
- 1888 Jamming
- 1894 Grinding
- 1895 Jottling
- 1895 Mounting
- 1897 Pushing
- 1897 Putting (it in)
- 1897 Riding

1900s:
- 1923 Screwing
- 1928 Laying
- 1966 Drilling
- 1974 Jabbing

2000s:
- 2008 Pumping

THE ACT OF INTERCOURSE

1400s:

1400 A union
1450 Venery (The delights of venery, engaged in venery)
1470 Copulation
1480 A coupling

1500s:

1568 A fuck
1593 A stroke
1598 A roust

1600s:

1610 A pluck
1629 A frisk

1700s:

1705 A shove

1707 A poke
1741 A connection
1750 A conjunction
1780 A merry bout
1788 A mow
1788 A shag

1800s:

1838 A roger
1848 Coitus
1890 A bout
1895 A mount
1897 A poke
1897 A push
1897 A ride

1900s:

1928 A lay
1929 A screw

SEMEN

1500s:

1500 Milk
1530 Discharge
1530 Emissions
1598 Marrow

1600s:

1600 Seed
1608 Mettle
1608 Stuff
1629 Cream
1635 Roe
1650 Proceedings
1650 Semen
1660 Fluid
1670 Contributions

1700s:

1748 Injection

1800s:

1840 Inpourings
1840 Tallow
1842 Paste
1870 Spunk
1879 Spend
1888 Jism

1900s:

1900 Goo
1915 Load
1923 Cum
1930 Wad
1935 Love juice
1957 Jizz
1965 Custard
1972 Sauce
1987 Spooge
1989 Spew
1995 Nectar
1997 Nut

2000s:

2003 Batter

VAGINAL DISCHARGE

1300s:
- 1350 moisture
- 1350 wetness

1500s:
- 1530 Emissions
- 1548 Quim

1600s:
- 1603 Curds

1800s:
- 1882 Love juice
- 1884 Cream

1900s:

1939 Drool
1948 Cum
1967 Pussy liquid
1981 Cooze
1988 Pussy juice

PART 2: BARROOM, BEDROOM, AND PILLOW TALK

LOVER

TRUE LOVE

1100s:
- 1175 Dear

1200s:
- 1200 Spouse
- 1206 Husband/Wife
- 1225 Lover

1300s:
- 1300 Loved one
- 1398 Beloved

1500s:
- 1503 Paramour
- 1573 Mate

1576 Sweetheart/Sweetie
1596 Darling

1700s:
1749 Partner

1800s:
1822 Boyfriend/Girlfriend
1839 Baby

1900s:
1906 Honey/Hon
1942 Pumpkin
1969 Dom(me)/Sub
1970 Master/Slave (a consenting relationship)

SNOG PARTNER

1500s:
1550 Companion

1900s:
1970 Fuck buddy
1995 Friend with benefits

OBJECTIFICATION

1300s:
1300 Conquerer/Conquest
1300 Master/Slave (without consent)

1375 Slut

1500s:
- 1500 Victim
- 1530 Breeder
- 1530 Whore

1700s:
- 1750 Instrument
- 1750 Assailant of choice

2000s:
- 2005 Cum bucket
- 2005 Cum dumpster

HEAD

1500s:

- 1508 Noddle
- 1522 Crag
- 1522 Noll
- 1567 Sconce

1600s:

- 1608 Block
- 1698 Nob

1700s:

- 1733 Dome
- 1785 Napper
- 1786 Box
- 1796 Can

1800s:

- 1803 Attic
- 1803 Noodle
- 1831 Conk
- 1837 Gourd
- 1838 Machinery
- 1842 Pumpkin
- 1858 Cabeza
- 1859 Lob
- 1859 Noggin
- 1861 Roof
- 1865 Chump
- 1868 Melon
- 1895 Think-box
- 1897 Belfry
- 1899 Lid

1900s:

- 1901 Loft
- 1908 Bean
- 1908 Coop
- 1911 Balloon
- 1915 Pan
- 1915 Cauliflower
- 1920 Acorn
- 1921 Egg
- 1930 Derby
- 1931 Barney
- 1931 Top
- 1938 Squash
- 1944 Chimney
- 1955 Casaba

1956 Nodder
1963 Nutter

2000s:
2003 Nana
2011 Tin can
2011 Wigwam

HAIR

1500s:

- 1551 Poll

1900s:

- 1960 Pez
- 1979 Head-top

EYES

1500s:

- 1561 Peepers
- 1589 Spies
- 1593 Lamps

1600s:

- 1619 Optics
- 1636 Goggles
- 1654 Twinklers
- 1673 Ogles

1700s:

- 1746 Sparklers
- 1747 Peeps
- 1754 Sees
- 1797 Blinkers

1800s:

1814 Glimmers
1820 Lights
1821 Skylights
1821 Winkers
1829 Headlights
1930 Squinters
1833 Gapers
1836 Lookouts
1847 Weepers
1858 Headlights
1858 Saucers
1860 Windows
1870 Blinks
1885 Shutters

1900s:

1903 Seers
1906 Squints
1913 Lookers
1917 Baby blues
1923 Peekers
1944 Spotters
1949 Bo-peeps
1954 Dimmers
1964 Pearls
1979 Beads
1990 Icy blues

MOUTH

1300s:
- 1367 Maw

1400s:
- 1426 Muzzle

1500s:
- 1550 Gob
- 1573 Wicket
- 1577 Chops

1600s:
- 1653 Clacker

1700s:
- 1700 Smoke hole

1722 Gab
1776 Trap
1785 Mummer

1800s:

1818 Chatterbox
1821 Box of ivories
1821 Chaffer
1825 Clam
1830 Gig
1830 Kissing trap
1832 Patterer
1835 Sauce box
1837 Beak
1840 Pan
1841 Sausage box
1845 Grub trap
1846 Blowhole
1855 Hopper
1860 Beefeater
1860 Whistler
1865 Busser
1880 Garret
1880 Yawp
1889 Grubber
1891 Puss
1895 Face

1900s:

1900 Cavern
1900 Wad
1902 Feeder

1903 Sluice
1908 Jib
1909 Chapper
1914 Gate
1942 Blabber
1945 Biter
1954 Flap
1957 Yack
1975 Tunnel
1986 Cocksucker
1988 Smacker

2000s:

2002 Screech
2005 Clap-trap

LIPS

1500s:

- 1577 Chops
- 1590 Chaps

1600s:

- 1665 Gans

1700s:

- 1786 Chaffers
- 1789 Lispers
- 1789 Mums

1800s:

- 1833 Clamshells

1900s:
- 1900 Flappers
- 1944 Gates
- 1947 Rubies

2000s:
- 2000 Cocksuckers

TONGUE

1500s:

1594 Clack

1600s:

1609 Clapper
1698 Red Rag
1698 Velvet

1700s:

1786 Chaffer

1800s:

1846 Tattler
1851 Lapper
1859 Jib
1864 Glib

1900s:

- 1900 Flapper
- 1926 Mouth organ
- 1972 Red carpet

2000s:

- 2002 Licker
- 2011 Ball licker

TEETH

1500s:

- 1598 Grinders

1600s:

- 1698 Snags

1700s:

- 1739 Fangs
- 1796 Ivories

1800s:

- 1811 Cogs
- 1820 Chatterers
- 1823 Nutcrackers
- 1824 Tusks
- 1845 Rails
- 1887 Crunchers

1892 Pearlies

1900s:

1902 Chewers
1912 Eaters
1915 Pearly whites
1923 Snappers
1930 Rocks
1944 Biters
1949 Choppers
1950 Chompers
1950 Clackers
1959 Chiclets
1961 Dentals
1964 Jibs
1970 Peggers
1978 Crackers
1995 Grill
1999 Clickers

2000s:

2001 Gnashers

CHIN AND NECK

CHIN

1900s:
: 1928 Whiskers

NECK

1500s:
: 1523 Crag

1700s:
: 1753 Scrag

1800s:
: 1835 Wiggen

1900s:

1903 Squeezer

THROAT

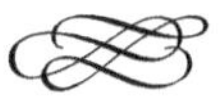

1300s:

- 1386 Whistle

1500s:

- 1573 Wicket

1600s:

- 1600 Organ pipe
- 1607 Gutter
- 1654 Guzzle
- 1693 Quail pipe

1700s:

- 1713 Funnel
- 1725 Throttle
- 1785 Swallow

1800s:

- 1832 Chaffer
- 1843 Red lane alley
- 1864 Peck alley
- 1891 Goozle
- 1893 Gin lane
- 1899 Gargler

1900s:

- 1902 Feeder
- 1909 Beer street
- 1918 Hatch
- 1933 Drain
- 1973 Swallow-pipe

2000s:

- 2012 Set of pipes

STOMACH

1600s:

- 1641 Crib

1700s:

- 1725 Crag
- 1753 Bread basket
- 1773 Pot

1800s:

- 1821 Middle
- 1824 Grubbery
- 1845 Pantry
- 1848 Tum
- 1850 Tummy
- 1859 Bingie
- 1889 Basket
- 1899 Boiler

1900s:

- 1902 Pod
- 1909 Pussy gut
- 1909 Puss-gut
- 1938 Flue
- 1965 Fuck handles
- 1969 Love handles
- 1998 Six pack

2000s:

- 2000 Eight pack

ARMS

1600s:
- 1674 Smiters

1700s:
- 1786 Rammers

1800s:
- 1812 Flippers
- 1823 Wings
- 1858 Drumsticks
- 1887 Props

1900s:
- 1917 Pump handles
- 1944 Flappers

HANDS AND FISTS

HANDS

1500s:

- 1551 Claws
- 1593 Paws

1600s:

- 1600 Pickers
- 1600 Stealers
- 1684 Friggers
- 1698 Fams

1700s:

- 1785 Clutches

1800s:

- 1800 Gropers

1811 Mawleys
1812 Mittens
1821 Nippers
1821 Scratchers
1823 Puds
1827 Graplers
1830 Plyers
1844 Feelers
1859 Dukes
1859 Grabbers
1869 Props
1881 Clampers
1893 Mitts

1900s:
1903 Shakers
1911 Hams
1911 Meat hooks
1919 Grub grabbers
1919 Grub hooks
1924 Pussy glommers
1942 Dry-mouthed widow
1942 Five-fingered widow
1964 Clam diggers
1965 Mrs. Palm (and her five daughters)
1966 Bread snatchers
1968 Dick skinners
1968 Five-fingered Annie
1969 Clams
1972 Rosy Palm (and her five sisters)
1976 Cock scratchers
1986 Mrs. Palmer (and her five daughters)
1988 Mrs. Hand

1997 Madam Palm (and her five sisters)
1999 Cunt scratchers
1999 Wanking spanners

2000s:
2001 Tit spanners
2011 Dick beaters

FISTS

1700s:
1790 Knuckle dabbers

1800s:
1812 Mittens
1816 Maulers
1822 Bones
1826 Fives
1847 Tippers
1869 Props
1880 Nutcrackers
1885 Dukes

1900s:
1981 Guns

LEGS AND KNEES

LEGS

1500s:

- 1512 Pins
- 1590 Hams

1700s:

- 1709 Spindles
- 1751 Timbers
- 1770 Drumsticks
- 1790 Gams

1800s:

- 1833 Supporters
- 1848 Underpinnings
- 1860 Stems
- 1881 Sticks

1900s:

1904 Uprights
1917 Hikers
1927 Bracers
1934 Toothpicks
1944 Twigs
1960 Choppers
1964 Poles
1980 Ham hocks

KNEES

1500s:

1532 Marybones
1567 Marrowbones

1700s:

1772 Knappers

1800s:

1870 Prayer handles
1877 Prayer bones

FEET AND TOES

FEET

1500s:

- 1557 Goers
- 1597 Hoofs

1600s:

- 1608 Walkers
- 1674 Stampers
- 1698 Trotters

1700s:

- 1790 Trampers

1800s:

- 1825 Padders
- 1838 Kickers

- 1848 Tootsies
- 1853 Steppers
- 1858 Shufflers
- 1878 Trots
- 1889 Creepers

1900s:

- 1908 Pedals
- 1928 Creeps
- 1928 Dancers
- 1944 Stomps
- 1944 Trods
- 1946 Crunchers
- 1949 Pads
- 1960 Barges

TOES

1900s:

- 1944 Wigglers

BODY

1800s:

- 1812 Frame
- 1825 Hulk
- 1834 Meat

1900s:

- 1930 Chassis
- 1947 Bod
- 1983 Structure

BREASTS

1200s:
- 1200 Bosom

1500s:
- 1507 Paps

1600s:
- 1608 Ivory balls
- 1610 Apples
- 1654 Globes
- 1674 Heavers
- 1681 Boobies
- 1690 Snowballs

1700s:
- 1707 Dumplings
- 1708 Udders

1731 Plumpers
1770 Bags
1788 Titties

1800s:
1826 Boobs
1862 Tits
1888 Pair
1890 Knockers

1900s:
1909 Coconuts
1916 Milkshakes
1920 Honeydews
1925 Briskets
1928 Bazooms
1929 Pippins
1932 Eyes
1932 Stacked
1935 Milkers
1939 Casabas
1939 Rack
1940 Equipment
1940 Maracas
1942 Bonbons
1942 Doodads
1942 Melons
1945 Bobbers
1952 Hooters
1957 Jugs
1959 Cans
1963 Balls

1963 Bazookas
1963 Fun bags
1963 Headlights
1963 Puppies
1963 Stack
1964 Cantaloupes
1966 Bee stings
1966 Watermelons
1967 Grapefruit
1967 Chugs
1967 Nippers
1967 Whoppers
1972 Bazongas
1974 Glands
1975 Balloons
1976 Mosquito bites
1978 Johnsons
1980 Grapes
1983 Mountains
1983 Tatas
1985 Bazoombas
1986 Bongos
1987 Jigglers
1987 Mangos
1988 Bouncers
1997 Cahoonas

2000s:

2000 Airbags
2002 Fuck udders
2002 Honkers
2003 Shirt stretchers

MALE GENITALS

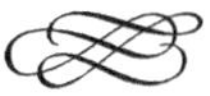

PARTS OF THE PENIS (TOP TO BOTTOM)

Head
- Tip
- Tiny slit
- Prepuce (foreskin)
- Shaft
- Base
- Roots
- Sack
- Testicles

FULL GENITALS

1400s:
- 1465 Jewels

1500s:
- 1520 Gear

1533 Tackle
1546 Giblets

1600s:
1629 Trinkets
1654 It
1660 Billiard Balls and stick
1663 Musket and bandeliers
1696 Wedding tackle

1700s:
1702 Scut
1707 Charms
1720 Rule of three
1790 Bellows

1800s:
1890 Accoutrements
1890 Equipment
1895 Credentials

1900s:
1922 Goods
1934 Tiddley push
1935 Three-piece set
1940 Particulars
1941 Basket
1942 Gadgets
1958 Whatsits
1965 Groceries

1966 Crown Jewels
1966 Wedding kit
1969 Nards
1970 Bunch
1970 Gonies
1972 Baggage
1972 Package
1972 Scepter and jewels
1979 The lot
1984 Wedding gear
1986 Machinery
1989 Fruit salad
1990 Pooney
1990 Tricky bits
1992 Lunchbox
1997 Junk
1998 Cricket set
1998 Stoggs

2000s:

2001 String and nuggets
2003 Picnic basket

PENIS

1400s:

- 1460 Pin
- 1499 Clicket
- 1499 Lance

1500s:

- 1500 Cod
- 1500 Instrument
- 1523 Fiddle
- 1533 Iron
- 1540 Tool
- 1540 Yard
- 1550 Pen
- 1560 Prick
- 1573 Pike
- 1580 Manhood
- 1580 Plough
- 1590 Weapon
- 1591 Rod

1593 Bauble
1593 Worm

1600s:
1603 Beef
1604 Jack
1605 Joint
1606 Needle
1607 Pole
1613 Stump
1614 Inch
1619 Cock
1620 Quill
1623 Sting
1625 Column
1638 Awl
1653 Bush beater
1653 Flip flap
1653 Roger
1653 Rump splitter
1653 Spigot
1653 Staff
1664 Drum
1670 Shuttle
1670 Whore pipe
1684 Frigger
1684 Ranger
1686 Knick-knack
1691 Pikestaff

1700s:
1700 Truncheon

1701 Plugtail
1719 Spicket
1720 Flute
1730 Pump handle
1732 Arbor
1741 Jock
1750 Throbbing mass
1763 Pointer
1763 Stallion
1768 Ramrod
1768 Thomas
1772 Shaft
1775 Dagger
1780 Gland
1785 Doodle
1786 Tube
1793 Dirk
1797 Sconce

1800s:

1816 Poker
1830 Engine
1833 Johnny
1836 Dick
1836 Prong
1837 Musket
1837 Nob
1843 Rod
1846 Agitator
1850 Broomstick
1850 Power
1860 Roly-poly
1860 William

1863 Johnson
1863 Trouser serpent
1865 Schlong
1865 Tallywag
1880 Love stick
1884 Torch
1888 Cucumber
1888 Cunt plugger
1888 Cunt stopper
1888 Cunt stretcher
1888 Spouter
1890 Abraham
1890 Arse opener
1890 Arse wedge
1890 Bayonet
1890 Beard splitter
1890 Bludgeon
1890 Bum tickler
1890 Bush whacker
1890 Butcher
1890 Crack hunter
1890 Cranny hunter
1890 Creamstick
1890 Cutlass
1890 Dart
1890 Diddle
1890 Dingus
1890 Doodle
1890 Flapdoodle
1890 Fornicator
1890 Gooser
1890 Gravy maker
1890 Grinding tool
1890 Gutstick

1890 Hunter
1890 Jacob
1890 Jigger
1890 Kit
1890 Little Davy
1890 Lodger
1890 Man root
1890 Member
1890 Merry maker
1890 Pendulum
1890 Pile driver
1890 Quim stake
1890 Quim wedge
1890 Radish
1890 Tent peg
1890 Winkle
1896 Lob
1896 Quit stick

1900s:

1904 Majesty
1905 Ding-dong
1914 Whanger
1915 Axe
1916 Dingle
1916 Drill
1916 Joystick
1916 Nightstick
1916 Pencil
1920 Cob
1920 Wee-wee
1922 Jerry
1922 Tickler

1924 Banana
1925 Hot dog
1925 Okra
1927 Patootie
1927 Pee-pee
1928 Candystick
1928 Organ grinder
1934 Putz
1934 Whang
1935 Toothpick
1935 Wiener
1939 Weenie
1941 Birdie
1942 Gadget
1947 Length
1948 Wong
1950 Tinker
1958 Fuck stick
1963 Gaff
1965 Log
1965 Muscle
1965 Whistle
1965 Yang
1966 Sticker
1966 Thingy
1967 Gong
1967 Rodney
1967 Salami
1967 Willie/Willy
1968 Choad
1969 Bell rope
1971 Unit
1972 Candy cane
1972 Cherry splitter

1972 Clam spear
1972 Ding-a-ling
1972 Dinky
1972 One-eyed monster
1972 Python
1972 Shovel
1972 Stud
1972 Third leg
1974 Knockwurst
1975 Noodle
1978 Crank
1978 Enchilada
1978 Tree
1982 Pug
1984 Love pump
1986 Mr. Happy
1987 Boner
1987 Bozack
1988 Jim/Jimmy
1988 Popsicle
1994 Nozzle
1994 Twinkie
1997 Love torpedo
1997 Scallywag
1997 Tockley
1998 Dobber
1998 Tootle

2000s:

2000 Trouser snake
2001 Butt plunger
2001 Cunt hook
2001 Dode

2001 Meat stick
2001 Twig
2001 Welt
2002 Man muscle
2002 Saucepan handle
2003 Jazz rocket
2003 Oboe
2003 Rover
2011 Jammer
2016 Soldier

TESTICLES

1300s:
- 1366 Ballocks

1400s:
- 1460 Ballock-stones
- 1460 Stones
- 1466 Eggs

1500s:
- 1508 Balls
- 1566 Cods
- 1597 Bullets

1600s:
- 1618 Plums
- 1620 Pebbles
- 1637 Culls

1653 Cullions
1680 Tarriwags
1682 Purse
1684 Nutmegs
1696 Pair

1700s:
1732 Bags
1760 Baggage
1762 Oysters
1785 Bawbels
1785 Tallywags
1785 Whiffles
1788 Drummers
1788 Twiddle-diddles
1790 Hammers

1800s:
1834 Apples
1837 Knackers
1837 Nuts
1837 Periwinkle
1879 Bollox
1888 Ball bag
1889 Bobbles
1889 Sack
1890 Jelly bag
1890 Nick-nacks

1900s:
1916 Marbles

1918 Glands
1930 Nerts
1932 Cojones
1934 Danglers
1948 Rocks
1960 Diamonds
1962 Winkie
1963 Apricots
1963 Nuggets
1964 Nads
1967 Cubes
1968 Swingers
1970 Chimes
1971 Nutsack
1972 Knick-knack
1973 Jewels
1973 Orbs
1975 Acorns
1979 Seedbag
1980 Gooseberries
1982 Berries
1988 Huevos
1992 Nad bag
1993 Coconuts
1995 Gold nuggets
1997 Choad
1997 Jizz bag
1997 Raisin bag
1997 Saddlebag
1998 Maracas
1999 Clankers
1999 Grapes

2000s:

- 2000 Bojangles
- 2000 Grollies
- 2001 Bitch bag
- 2001 Dick sack
- 2001 Satch
- 2001 Satchel
- 2003 Bollock bag
- 2008 Nut bag

ERECT PENIS

1500s:

1589 Come aloft
1597 Standing

1600s:

1606 Stalk
1650 Stiff stander
1653 Stiff and stout
1654 Standing ague
1660 Stand
1680 Cocked

1700s:

1785 Horn colic
1788 Piss proud

1800s:

1840 Baton
1842 Spike
1864 Hard-on
1879 Cockstand
1881 Rise
1888 Stiff (having a bit of stiff)
1890 Bayonet
1890 Broom handle
1890 Hard bit
1890 Jack
1895 Roaring Jack
1896 Horn

1900s:

1904 Swelling
1935 Get it up
1935 Lift
1940 Roger
1944 Woodie
1945 Stand-on
1958 Boner
1963 Rod-on
1963 Whopper
1966 Bar
1966 Bar-up
1966 On the hard
1967 Flag
1968 Stiffy
1969 Early morn
1970 Jack handle
1970 Rail
1971 Hard-up

1972 Booboo
1972 Jackhammer
1972 Pinky
1972 Pride of the morning
1975 Blue veiner
1975 Diamond cutter
1975 Ten-hut
1981 Bone ache
1981 Semi
1987 Stonker
1991 Bugle
1992 Guided missile
1992 Sprung
1993 Wood
1993 Morning wood
1997 Get wood
1997 Pan handle
1998 Stiffer
1999 Stand to attention
1999 Stiff lock

2000s:

2000 Bone up
2001 Morning glory
2001 Pocket rocket
2001 Rocky
2004 Log
2005 Truncheon

LARGE PENIS

1600s:

1620 Hung
1682 Lobcock

1700s:

1748 Stretcher

1800s:

1979 Tosser
1888 Belly tickler
1888 Donkey prick
1888 Hair curler
1888 Kidney wiper
1888 Liver lifter

1900s:

1927 Kidney cracker

1928 Hose
1930 Kidney prodder
1935 Kidney buster
1935 Tonsil tickler
1950 Sollicker
1952 Kidney washer
1963 Whopper
1969 Womb beater
1970 Donkey dick
1972 Batter
1972 Dangler
1972 Honker
1972 Stacked
1979 Womb sweeper
1988 Horse meat
1989 Dragon
1994 Packing

2000s:

2000 Horse-cocked
2001 Kidney scraper

VAGINA

1300s:

- 1325 Cunt
- 1367 Tail
- 1386 Belle-chose
- 1386 Quaint
- 1386 Quoniam

1400s:

- 1465 Socket
- 1495 Lap
- 1495 Trench
- 1499 Clicket-gate

1500s:

- 1517 Token
- 1520 Oven
- 1533 Mill
- 1538 Dock

1538 Pudding
1538 Purse
1540 Pin case
1546 Jewel
1550 Quiver
1564 Gulf
1566 Fort
1567 Saddle
1568 Pit
1575 Commodity
1580 Sheath
1584 Altar of Venus
1590 Lips
1591 Cunny hole
1591 Netherlands
1591 Venus's cradle
1592 Fountain
1592 Pitcher
1593 Placket
1594 Honey pot
1594 Ring
1595 Eye
1598 Nock
1599 Cunny

1600s:

1600 Nest
1600 Nonny
1600 Rose
1600 Womb
1602 Muff
1604 Gap
1606 Case

1606 Venus's court
1607 Keyhole
1607 Lute
1607 Trinket
1608 Ditch
1609 Orchard
1611 Notch
1612 Furrow
1614 Engine
1615 Dish
1616 Kettle
1620 Flue
1620 Garden
1628 Tinderbox
1640 Slit
1646 Lower mouth
1650 Cunnigate
1650 Vitals
1653 Flapdoodle
1655 Loom
1656 Nether lips
1656 Twat
1656 Cauldron
1657 Fancy
1660 Orifice
1661 Tub
1670 Placket box
1671 Cunny alley
1671 Cunny hall
1673 Alcove
1673 Lapland
1675 Pin box
1680 Altar
1680 Cloven spot

1680 Cupid's warehouse
1681 Cunny burrow
1682 Taft
1683 Entrance
1683 Premises
1685 Kitchen
1690 Crack
1698 Cellar

1700s:

1700 Cupid's feast
1700 Sluice
1705 Butter box
1705 Forge
1705 Love's cabinet
1705 Quim
1707 Garden of Venus
1709 Quiff
1718 Till
1718 Spunk box
1719 Kitty
1719 Venus's honeypot
1721 Cockloft
1724 Milking pail
1732 Sex
1740 Shell
1748 Cleft
1748 Cockpit
1748 Nether-mouth
1750 Trot
1759 Placket hole
1768 Quin
1772 Cradle

1775 Shrine of Venus
1784 Burrow
1785 Cauliflower
1785 Cock alley
1785 Mantrap
1785 Snatch
1785 Waterworks
1786 Doodle sack
1786 Charms
1786 Gash
1797 Grove of Venus

1800s:

1801 Temple of Venus
1808 Merry bit
1821 Pin cushion
1826 Gulf of Venus
1833 Crib
1833 Locker
1833 Tunnel
1834 Belly
1836 Crevice
1836 Dolly
1836 Jewel case
1836 Pail
1836 Snatch box
1836 Spigot hole
1837 Down below
1840 Quint
1840 Twitcher
1841 Lucky bag
1841 Tulip
1843 Clam

1864 Spout
1879 Pussy
1879 Quimmy
1880 Pokehole
1884 Jam
1885 Shagging machine
1888 Coo
1888 Front entrance
1888 Moistened aperture
1888 Motte
1888 Sperm sucker
1889 Groove
1890 Belly entrance
1890 Bit of jam
1890 Bit of snug
1890 Cupid's anvil
1890 Downy bit
1890 Garden of Eden
1891 Cabbage
1891 Cauldron
1891 Cave
1891 Cellar
1891 Cock chafer
1891 Cock holder
1891 Cock inn
1891 Cookie
1891 Cream jug
1892 Chasm
1892 Flap
1892 Fuckhole
1892 Gravy giver
1892 Gully
1892 Gutter
1892 Hairy ring

1892 Heaven
1892 Magnet
1896 Fleshpot
1896 The ineffable
1896 Jam pot
1896 Jelly bag
1896 Knick knack
1896 Lather maker

1900s:
1900 Pussycat
1902 Naggie
1902 Naughty
1902 Pen wiper
1902 Pintle case
1902 Prick holder
1902 Prick hole
1902 Prick purse
1902 Prick skinner
1903 Seminary
1903 Shakebag
1903 South Pole
1903 Spew alley
1903 Split apricot
1903 Split fig
1903 Split mutton
1903 Suck-and-swallow
1904 Tail gap
1904 Tail gate
1904 Tail hole
1904 Target
1904 Tickler
1904 Undertaker

1904 Underworld
1904 Upright grin
1904 Vestry
1916 Bearded oyster
1920 Satchel
1923 Pantry
1925 Twitchet
1927 Beaver
1927 Bit of tail
1927 Jewelry
1928 Downtown
1929 Sweet potato pie
1933 Doughnut
1934 Boogie-woogie
1935 Coffee spout
1935 Gravy bowl
1935 Heater
1935 Minge
1939 Grinding mill
1939 Joy hole
1947 Coffee grinder
1947 Cush
1947 Poontang
1951 Pom pom
1952 Shunt
1956 Great divide
1958 Goodie
1961 Apple
1962 Sausage grinder
1963 Furburger
1963 Furry hoop
1963 Garage
1963 Snake gully
1966 Bearded clam

1966 Bearded lady
1966 Bearded taco
1966 Cooch
1966 Happy valley
1966 Hot box
1966 Poonce
1966 Slash
1966 Snake pit
1966 Toolbox
1967 Parking lot
1968 Poon
1969 Muffin
1971 Snapper
1971 Vertical smile
1972 Nookie
1974 Bumper
1974 La la
1975 Unit
1980 Pole hole
1980 Pussy hole
1983 Maw
1985 Package
1986 Bamba
1986 Cooter
1986 Flower patch
1992 Dugout
1992 In-between
1992 Slice
1995 Hairy bank
1995 Kitten
1996 Hairy molly
1996 Pokey
1997 Giblets
1997 Hairy cup

1997 Hairy doughnut
1997 Hairy goblet
1997 Pootie
1997 Spasm chasm
1999 Tomato

2000s:

2000 Hidden forest
2000 Lily
2000 Shag bag
2000 Snicket
2001 Lunchbox
2001 Trap
2001 Trickle
2002 Basket
2003 Batcave
2003 Burger
2005 Credentials
2005 Love shack
2010 Moot
2014 Vajiggle-jaggle / Va J-J

FEMALE GENITALS

CLIT

1600s:

- 1600 Nub
- 1680 Clit
- 1680 Clitoris

1900s:

- 1909 Cockey
- 1916 Boy in the boat
- 1962 Dick
- 1966 Dot
- 1972 Joy button
- 1972 Man in the boat
- 1974 Dingleberry
- 1980 Little ploughman
- 1982 Cockpit
- 1982 Joy buzzer
- 1983 Tastebud

1997 Bald man in the boat
1999 Love button

2000s:
2000 Baby in the boat
2007 Pearl

LABIA

1600s:
1604 Nonny-nonny
1630 Folds
1650 Door

1800s:
1888 Cunt lips
1888 Flags
1888 Flaps
1888 Flappers
1888 Twats

1900s:
1950 Grinning bear
1959 Curtains
1960 Jaws
1967 Gapper
1980 Ear between the legs
1988 Mutton flaps
1990 Labes
1997 Camel's foot
1998 Fanny flaps

2000s:

2000 Dew flaps
2001 Camel toe
2002 Fuck flaps
2003 Sushi taco
2003 Tuna taco

PUBIC HAIR

1500s:

1525 Beard
1593 Fur
1595 Bird's nest
1597 Bearskin

1600s:

1600 Bush
1638 Moss
1659 Forest
1659 Thicket
1660 Tuft
1665 Muff

1700s:

1772 Stubble
1788 Tabby
1797 Brush

1800s:

1833 Thatch
1844 Hair

1864 Shrubs
1875 Fluff
1880 Fuzz
1883 Plush
1885 Quim whiskers
1888 Fleece
1888 Pussy
1890 Belly whiskers
1890 Broom
1890 Down
1890 Nether whiskers
1890 Shrubbery

1900s:

1927 Beaver
1939 Rug
1939 Whiskers
1942 Mop
1953 Cunt hair
1960 Pussy hair
1966 Briar patch
1966 Garden
1966 Lawn
1969 Trim
1980 Snatch thatch
1982 Chuff
1982 Velvet

2000s:

2000 Hedge
2006 Minge

THE ACT OF CUNNILINGUS

1700s:

1744 A larking

1800s:

1888 A cunt-licking
1888 An eating
1895 A face job
1898 A sucking

1900s:

1927 A pearl dive
1927 A tongue lap
1928 A deep-sea dive
1928 Diving the bush
1928 Going downtown
1930 A Pearl fishing
1934 Getting down on it
1934 Gobbling the gravy

1934 Sucking off
1939 Eating hair pie
1939 Eating pussy
1939 A high dive
1941 A gash eating
1941 Go down south
1943 Muffing
1946 Chewing
1949 A muff dive
1950 Going in the bush
1963 Dining at the Y
1963 Lap it up
1964 Sitting on his face
1965 A licking out
1965 A lip reading
1965 A scarfing
1965 A tongue job
1966 A box lunch
1966 A bush dinner
1967 A fressing
1968 A cop
1969 Eating her out
1969 A plating
1971 A muff job
1971 A pussy eating
1972 A cunt lapping
1972 A cunt sucking
1972 A gash guzzling
1972 A lick
1972 A lap loving
1980 Eating pie
1980 A freak fucking
1982 A beard ride
1983 Dipping in the bush

1985 Eating her flowers
1985 Eating taffy
1988 Eating fur pie
1988 Eating furburger
1989 A carpet licking
1989 A carpet munching
1989 A muff dive
1989 A rug munching
1989 A tongue pie
1997 A blow job
1997 A chow down
1999 A clam dive

2000s:

2000 A muff munching
2000 Munching the box
2002 Chewing bubblegum
2002 Cleaning the carpet
2002 Licking the box

ONE WHO PERFORMS CUNNILINGUS

1800s:

1890 A face man

1900s:

1916 A cunt lapper
1928 A deep-sea diver
1929 A muff diver
1941 A gash eater
1942 A cunt licker
1942 A cunt sucker
1960 A muffer
1965 A lip reader
1966 A cat lapper
1967 A fresser
1967 A pussy kisser
1969 A pussy licker
1971 A pussy eater
1971 A pussy lapper
1972 A gash guzzler

1988 A minge muncher
1989 A carpet muncher
1989 A pebble licker
1989 A rug muncher

2000s:
2000 A muff muncher
2003 A box biter
2003 A bush licker

THE ACT OF FELLATIO

1700s:

1744 A larking

1800s:

1873 A mouth fuck
1879 A cocksucking
1879 A minetting
1898 A prick eating

1900s:

1905 A suck off
1927 A tongue-lapping
1929 A sucking
1935 A French bath
1940 A cocksuck
1941 A suck
1941 A tongue bath
1946 A blow

1948 A blow job
1948 A tongue party
1949 A b.j.
1951 A header
1954 A gam
1960 A smoker
1960 A snow job
1965 A gum job
1965 A head job
1965 A hum job
1965 A prick-sucking
1965 A tongue job
1969 A derby
1969 A plate
1969 Plating
1970 A job
1971 A hummer
1971 A man-eating
1971 A pipe job
1971 A skull job
1972 An ice job
1972 A knob job
1972 A kowtow chow
1972 A mouth job
1972 Polishing the knob
1972 A quickie
1972 A salt seller
1972 A shore dinner
1972 A zipper dinner
1972 Zipper sex
1973 Deep throat
1975 A hat job
1975 A sucky-sucky
1976 A lip lock

1976 A lock lip
1980 A knob-gobbling
1982 A polish
1987 A hose job
1988 A dick lick
1988 A face pussy
1988 A gob job
1989 A gobbling
1989 A knobber
1992 Lip action
1993 A skull fuck
1995 A polish and shine
1995 A shine
1998 A nosh
1999 Munching the truncheon
1999 A pickle-chugging

2000s:

2000 A boss
2000 A horn-smoking
2000 A lick and a shine
2000 A neck bone
2000 A spam supper
2002 A face-fucking
2003 A milkshake
2003 A suck job
2003 A white-mouthing
2011 A slurp

ONE WHO PERFORMS FELLATIO

1600s:

- 1611 A lick spigot

1800s:

- 1890 Cocksucker
- 1890 Spigot sucker
- 1890 Suckster
- 1890 Suckstress

1900s:

- 1904 Fluter
- 1917 Head worker
- 1920 Peter eater
- 1928 Face artist
- 1928 Muzzle
- 1934 Dicky licker
- 1934 Lapper
- 1941 Icing expert

1941 Mouth queen
1941 Mouth worker
1944 Head chick
1950 Nibbler
1960 Smoker
1962 Cum freak
1965 Goop gobbler
1965 Skin diver
1965 Sword swallower
1968 Dick licker
1971 Bone queen
1971 Dick eater
1971 Head artist
1971 Scum sucker
1972 Flute player
1972 Man eater
1972 Whistler
1977 Blowjob artist
1977 Dick chewer
1978 Clarinet player
1978 A nosher
1980 Knob gobbler
1982 A plater
1986 Prick sucker
1992 Cum chum
1992 Peter puffer
1992 Semen demon
1993 Choad smoker
1993 Pickle kisser
1993 Spunk gobbler
1995 A facialist
1996 Sperm burper
1997 Cock smoker
1997 Pipe smoker

1999 Cum chugger
1999 Pickle chugger

2000s:
2000 Dick sucker
2000 Horn smoker
2002 Bat sucker
2002 A spunk gullet
2003 Cum queen
2007 Pole smoker
2008 Dick smoker

ASS

1300s:

- 1363 Bum
- 1376 Arse

1500s:

- 1512 Prat
- 1533 Backside
- 1568 Behind
- 1576 Buttocks
- 1578 Crupper
- 1590 Stern

1600s:

- 1607 Cheeks
- 1650 Hillocks
- 1690 Netherend

1700s:

- 1761 Ass
- 1768 Rear
- 1774 Derrière
- 1777 Posterior
- 1794 Bottom

1800s:

- 1812 Nancy
- 1821 Bunt
- 1835 Duff
- 1835 Flanky
- 1849 Hindside
- 1889 Dopey

1900s:

- 1906 Crumpet
- 1923 Heinie
- 1926 Booty
- 1928 Bustle
- 1931 Hoochie coocher
- 1935 Tangerine
- 1941 Poundcake
- 1942 Bam-bam
- 1943 Backland
- 1943 Dinger
- 1946 Duster
- 1951 Buns
- 1958 Tush
- 1966 Backyard
- 1966 Seater
- 1967 Culo

1967 Cushion
1972 Flipside
1984 Glutes
1988 Sweetcheeks
1989 Porch
1990 Bum crack
1993 Back
1993 Tushy
1994 Can
1995 Bumper
1997 Butt crack
1999 Kazebo
1999 Kazoo

RECTUM

1400s:

- 1400 Arsehole

1500s:

- 1533 Nock
- 1535 Channel
- 1592 Backdoor
- 1594 Anus

1600s:

- 1604 Wind instrument
- 1611 Bunghole
- 1629 Shithole
- 1653 Nockhole
- 1664 Porthole
- 1681 Bum
- 1682 Back gate

1700s:

1701 Bum fiddle
1704 Grope hole
1720 Fugo
1725 Rectum
1726 Windward passage
1788 Back avenue
1790 Crevice

1800s:

1811 Round mouth
1838 Crack
1860 South Pole
1865 Asshole
1866 Bumhole
1888 Back entrance
1888 Pooper
1890 Ring

1900s:

1916 Cornhole
1925 Kite
1927 Brownie
1927 Farter
1927 Flue
1930 Keister
1934 Alley
1934 Tail
1942 Butthole
1945 Back
1945 Chute
1947 Blowhole

1959 Dot
1959 Patootie
1962 Satchel
1967 Red eye
1967 Ring piece
1971 Eye
1972 Alleyway
1973 Hershey highway
1976 Where the sun don't shine
1983 Back slit
1989 Back porch
1989 Winkle
1998 Tailpipe
1999 Abyss

2000s:
2000 Starfish / Pink starfish
2003 Ream
2011 Back alley

ANAL SEX

1500s:

1500 Up her bowels
1598 Bardash

1600s:

1675 Fuck

1700s:

1732 Graft
1744 Gig

1800s:

1800 Buried in her entrails
1874 Up her bowels
1879 Bumfuck
1879 Stuff
1880 Cornhole

1888 Backscuttle

1900s:

1908 Booger
1912 Moon
1925 Take it up the ass
1927 Snag
1930 Bunk up
1940 Browneye
1944 Dogpaddle
1949 Goose
1949 Punk
1950 Prat
1950 Seat
1952 Pogue
1962 Pack
1965 Buttbang
1965 Buttfuck
1965 Jook
1965 Thread
1966 Bottle
1967 Punk out
1970 Bum
1971 Saddle
1971 Swap out
1972 Buff
1972 Hit the round brown
1972 Jog
1972 Pack the mud
1972 Powder her cheeks
1972 Punch it
1972 Rectify
1973 Back a tail

1975 Backskull
1977 Flip flop
1979 Freak
1980 Dogfuck
1980 Freak fuck
1980 Rump
1980 Shoot in the tail
1981 Keister stab
1984 Backdoor
1985 Corndog
1989 Brown hole
1989 Bufu
1989 Dip in the fudge pot
1989 Fluff the duff
1990 Jazz
1994 Bone
1994 Dick
1994 Prong
1996 Jam
1999 Buke

2000s:
2001 Caboose
2002 Grease her keister
2003 Burgle
2003 Split the peach
2004 Bust her ass

DESCRIPTION OF INTERCOURSE – GERUNDS

1300s:

1380 Swiving

1500s:

1509 Dancing
1520 Clipping
1544 Occupying
1560 Juggling
1560 Pleasuring
1568 Fucking
1572 Smocking
1572 Treading
1590 Bobbing
1593 Stroking
1597 Stabbing
1598 Rousting
1598 Grinding

1600s:

1600 Jumbling
1600 Nimbling
1608 Niggling
1610 Wapping
1611 Fadoodling
1612 Prigging
1619 Clicketing
1629 Frisking
1633 Doing
1635 In and in
1642 Shifting
1654 Blowing
1654 Knocking
1660 Frigging
1673 Salting
1680 Shogging
1698 Strapping

1700s:

1703 Buttocking
1705 Shoving
1705 Stitching
1707 Poking
1712 Jerking
1720 Jobbing
1725 Nobbing
1738 Stuffing
1751 Touzling
1788 Mowing
1788 Shagging
1795 Fuddling

1797 Brushing

1800s:

1804 Quilting
1811 Relishing
1818 Strumming
1834 Trouncing
1837 Bundling
1837 Shooting
1840 Poking
1887 Ballocking
1887 Cunt plugging
1887 Injecting
1888 Jamming
1888 Ruddling
1888 Tailing
1890 Beard splitting
1890 Belly bumping
1892 Chawing
1892 Cock fighting
1892 Cunny catching
1892 Doodling
1893 Ferreting
1893 Fleshing it
1894 Goosing
1894 Grinding
1894 Intruding
1895 Hoisting
1895 Jottling
1895 Jumming
1895 Leaping
1895 Leather stretching

1895 Molrowing
1895 Motting
1895 Mounting
1895 Worrying (her insides)
1897 Pile driving
1897 Pushing
1897 Putting (it in)
1897 Quim sticking
1897 Quim wedging
1897 Riding
1897 Rump splitting
1897 Rumping
1897 Sewing
1897 Sliding
1899 Tail tickling
1899 Tromboning
1899 Tumbling
1899 Tummy tickling
1899 Twat raking
1899 Twat tickling
1899 Twatting

1900s:
1901 Vaulting
1901 Wiping
1905 Diddling
1918 Zig-zagging
1922 Rooting
1923 Screwing
1928 Jazzing
1928 Laying
1930 Switching
1950 Jacking

1960 Slicing
1966 Drilling
1974 Jabbing
1988 Bopping

2000s:
2008 Pumping

THE ACT OF INTERCOURSE

1400s:

1400 A union
1450 Venery (The delights of venery, engaged in venery)
1470 Copulation
1480 A coupling

1500s:

1509 A dance
1512 A sport
1568 A fuck
1590 A bob
1593 A stroke
1598 A roust

1600s:

1610 A jig
1610 A pluck
1626 A shot

1629 A frisk

1700s:

1705 A shove
1707 A poke
1712 A jerk
1725 A nub
1725 A wap
1741 A connection
1750 A conjunction
1780 A merry bout
1788 A mow
1788 A shag
1795 A fuddle
1797 A brush

1800s:

1837 A shoot
1838 A roger
1848 Coitus
1864 A grouse
1888 An injection
1889 A jam
1890 A bit
1890 A bout
1894 A grind
1895 A mount
1897 A poke
1897 A push
1897 A put
1897 A ride
1897 A rootle

1900s:

1927 A jazz
1928 A jive
1928 A lay
1929 A screw
1950 A jack
1950 A stab
1960 A slice
1974 A jab

SEMEN

1500s:

- 1500 Milk
- 1530 Discharge
- 1530 Emissions
- 1594 Butter
- 1598 Marrow

1600s:

- 1600 Seed
- 1608 Mettle
- 1608 Stuff
- 1610 Scad
- 1629 Cream
- 1635 Roe
- 1650 Proceedings
- 1650 Semen
- 1660 Fluid
- 1671 A dose
- 1670 Contributions

1673 Slime
1674 A flash in the pan
1685 Ammunition
1688 A squirter

1700s:
1748 Injection

1800s:
1800 Ointment
1837 Lather
1840 Inpourings
1840 Tallow
1842 Paste
1870 Spunk
1879 Spend
1888 Gruel
1888 Jism
1888 Muck
1888 Starch
1890 Dilberry
1890 Hot milk
1890 Letchwater
1890 Melted butter
1890 Milt
1890 Oyster
1890 Sugar
1890 Tail juice
1892 Snot
1896 Glue

1900s:

1900 Goo
1915 Load
1916 Spoof
1923 Cum
1927 Lump
1930 Wad
1932 Jazz
1934 Pearl drops
1935 Baby fluid
1935 Love juice
1936 Medicine
1942 Ammo
1944 Scum
1950 Pecker tracks
1957 Jizz
1961 Beer
1965 Custard
1965 Mess
1966 Comings
1970 Rice pudding
1972 Baby paste
1972 Face cream
1972 Felching
1972 Fruit juice
1972 Lube
1972 Pearls
1972 Sauce
1972 Snow storm
1972 Sticky
1979 Nelly
1980 Fetch
1980 Nature
1982 Jungle juice

1983 Axle grease
1983 Cheese
1987 Spooge
1988 Dick drink
1989 Spew
1989 Sploodge
1989 Spoo
1989 Spooch
1992 Skeeter
1993 Pearl necklace
1993 Spuff
1995 Nectar
1996 Snowball
1996 Spence
1997 Baby bullets
1997 Baby gravy
1997 Fuck sauce
1997 Nut
1997 Poontang
1997 Spud juice
1997 Tatty water
1997 White swallow
1999 Face paint
1999 Knob snot
1999 Melch
1999 Nut butter
1999 Tadpoles

2000s:

2000 Ballock gravy
2000 Ballock snot
2000 Cock snot
2000 Jizz water

2000 Love custard
2000 Nad jam
2000 Vinegar
2001 Dick splash
2001 Jip
2002 Cock sauce
2002 Spuzz
2003 Baff
2003 Ballock yoghurt
2003 Batter
2003 Come juice
2003 Pecker snot
2006 Man paste

VAGINAL DISCHARGE

1300s:

- 1350 moisture
- 1350 wetness

1500s:

- 1530 Emissions
- 1548 Quim

1600s:

- 1603 Curds
- 1661 Jelly

1800s:

- 1882 Love juice
- 1884 Cream
- 1884 Throw oil
- 1890 Goose grease

1892 Wax

1900s:

1939 Drool
1948 Cum
1963 Clam juice
1967 Pussy liquid
1981 Cooze
1982 Jungle juice
1983 Crotch cheese
1988 Pussy juice
1997 Fanny batter

2000s:

2000 Clam chowder
2000 Clitty litter
2000 Punta
2001 Poontang juice
2002 Bitch butter
2003 Clam jam
2003 Crotch oil
2003 Flap snot

BONUS: HISTORICAL VERBS AND EXCLAMATIONS!

TO MASTURBATE - VERBS

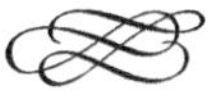

WOMAN

1600s:
- 1670 Frig

1700s:
- 1711 Masturbate

1900s:
- 1965 Finger fuck
- 1988 Diddle
- 1989 Jill off
- 1997 Thumb

MAN

1500s:
- 1598 Claw

1598 Frig
1598 Friggle
1598 Rub

1600s:
1610 Milk himself
1660 Toss off

1800s:
1800 Play himself off
1865 Jerk off
1879 Play with himself
1889 Jerk
1890 Shake himself
1898 Pull about

1900s:
1915 Diddle
1916 Bring off by hand
1916 Jack himself off
1919 Yank off
1930 Boff
1930 Splash himself
1940 Beat his meat
1948 Wank off
1949 Belt it
1950 Whack off
1960 Stroke
1962 Whack it
1965 Hand job
1966 Ball off

1966 Pump off
1966 Work himself off
1970 Yank
1971 Play with his stick
1972 Grind off
1972 Pound off
1972 Rub one off
1972 Screw off
1975 Yank it
1979 Rub it
1990 Pull himself off
1996 Bone it off
1996 Mess with himself
1996 Smack it off
1997 Squeeze one off

2000s:

2001 Frig off
2002 Bring himself off
2002 Slap it
2003 Squirt one off
2012 Fap

TO MASTURBATE - BAWDY VERSIONS INCLUDED

WOMAN

1600s:

1670 Frig

1700s:

1711 Masturbate

1900s:

1900 Sling her jelly
1965 Finger fuck
1988 Diddle fuck
1989 Jill off
1990 Flick the switch
1995 Floss the cat
1996 Poke her pussy
1997 Brush the beaver
1997 Thumb

1998 Apply the lip gloss

2000s:

2000 Glaze the donut
2000 Hit the slit
2000 Oil the glove
2001 Flick her bean
2002 Bury the knuckle
2002 Butter the muffin
2002 Fondle the fig
2002 Itch the ditch
2002 Juice the plum
2002 Play the beaver
2002 Play tiddlywinks
2002 Roll the marble
2002 Stir it up
2002 Stir the sauce
2003 Beat the beaver
2003 Clap her clit
2003 Grease the gash
2003 Pet her pussycat
2013 Smack the mackerel

MAN

1500s:

1598 Claw
1598 Frig
1598 Friggle
1598 Rub

1600s:

- 1610 Milk himself
- 1660 Toss off

1700s:

- 1785 Fetch mettle
- 1788 Stretch his pipe

1800s:

- 1800 Play himself off
- 1865 Jerk off
- 1879 Play with himself
- 1880 Pull his pudding
- 1888 Fuck his fist
- 1889 Jerk
- 1890 Shake himself
- 1898 Pull about

1900s:

- 1900 Sling his juice
- 1900 Shake himself up
- 1900 Shag himself
- 1904 Handle himself
- 1910 Pull his pud
- 1915 Diddle
- 1916 Bring off by hand
- 1916 Dub off
- 1916 Jack himself off
- 1919 Yank off
- 1920 Pull his plonker / plonk
- 1930 Boff

1930 Pull his duff
1930 Splash himself
1930 Whip the dummy
1931 Hand jig
1935 Belt his batter
1935 Flog the dummy
1938 Jerk his gherkin
1940 Beat his meat
1941 Bash it
1945 Pull his dick
1948 Wank off
1949 Belt it
1950 Bash the stick
1950 Beat the bishop
1950 Beat the dummy
1950 Beat the pup
1950 Whack off
1952 Flog his meat
1955 Flog the log
1955 Massage the frankfurter
1960 Stroke
1962 Whack it
1964 Pull his prick
1965 Hand job
1965 Jerk his mutton
1966 Ball off
1966 Pump off
1966 Work himself off
1967 Pull his cock
1970 Choke the lizard
1970 Polish his bayonet
1970 Pound his meat
1970 Whack his doodle
1970 Yank

1971 Play with his stick
1971 Stroke the lizard
1972 Grind off
1972 Knob polish
1972 Pound off
1972 Rub one off
1972 Screw off
1972 Shoot skeet
1975 Choke the chicken
1975 Yank it
1976 Flog his dong
1977 Pull on his meat
1977 Pump his meat
1979 Choke the gopher
1979 Rub it
1980 Flog the bishop
1980 Pump his pickle
1985 Milk the anaconda
1985 Spank the monkey
1985 Stroke the salami
1986 Bat himself off
1986 Wax his carrot
1987 Wax the dolphin
1990 Jerk his joint
1990 Pull himself off
1991 Clean his rifle
1991 Polish his knob
1992 Flog the log
1992 Kill some babies
1992 Pull the chain
1992 Yank his crank
1993 Doodle
1995 Flick the big
1995 Flip the bishop

1995 Free Willy
1996 Bone it off
1996 Cream his cock
1996 Juice the joystick
1996 Mess with himself
1996 Pump a gusher
1996 Smack it off
1997 Clear the custard
1997 Flick the dick
1997 Paint the ceiling
1997 Pull the pin
1997 Squeeze one off
1997 Squirt n' spurt
1997 Wank the crank
1997 Yank the plank
1998 Apply the handbrake
1998 Crank the shaft
1998 Unload the gun
1999 Download his floppy
1999 Pound the pork
1999 Slam the ham
1999 Tug the slug

2000s:

2000 Crack the bat
2000 Cream his beef
2000 Jack the corn
2000 Jack the joystick
2001 Flop one
2001 Frig off
2002 Beat the bologna
2002 Beat the dog
2002 Bring himself off

2002 Clean his pipes
2002 Jack his jazz
2002 Jack the sack
2002 Polish the bone
2002 Pump cream
2002 Slap it
2002 Strangle the snake
2002 Whack Willie
2003 Buff the banana
2003 Do the white knuckler
2003 Have a shower spank
2003 Shine the pole
2003 Slap the pud
2003 Slap the salami
2003 Squirt one off
2008 Choke the bishop
2012 Fap

THE ACT OF INTERCOURSE – VERBS

1400s:

- 1499 To clicket

1500s:

- 1505 To nug
- 1508 To fuck
- 1520 To clip
- 1520 To lay
- 1530 To sard
- 1538 To mow
- 1542 To occupy
- 1550 To chuck
- 1566 To niggle
- 1572 To smock
- 1572 To tread
- 1573 To stitch
- 1582 To bed
- 1591 To twig
- 1592 To mount

1593 To bob
1594 To hammer
1597 To charge
1597 To stab

1600s:

1600 To jerk
1600 To ram
1604 To work
1605 To please
1607 To jolt
1608 To cog
1608 To jog
1608 To shake
1610 To sluice
1610 To taste
1611 To cock
1611 To man
1611 To trim
1612 To buck
1612 To prig
1617 To drill
1619 To tug
1622 To ease
1622 To swinge
1629 To jig
1632 To diddle
1637 To split
1638 To hump
1642 To pluck
1642 To stroke
1648 To stump
1652 To sting

1655 To scour
1656 To wimble
1667 To fopdoodle
1670 To boff
1671 To shove
1674 To quiff
1675 To shift
1678 To bumble
1680 To bone
1680 To shag
1680 To stuff
1682 To drive
1682 To gallop
1683 To push
1684 To rake
1685 To bulk
1698 To brim
1698 To jock
1698 To strap
1698 To tiff

1700s:

1701 To pleasure
1703 To buttock
1705 To stitch
1710 To roger
1719 To cock it
1720 To flog
1730 To pump
1740 To wrap
1740 To yard
1751 To batter
1767 To switch

1771 To rump
1778 To tail
1785 To strum
1785 To touch up
1787 To bundle
1788 To snooze
1789 To nudge
1795 To fuddle
1797 To brush

1800s:

1820 To fondle
1833 To trounce
1835 To fix
1836 To cut
1840 To spit
1841 To roll
1851 To splice
1863 To get some
1869 To cross
1871 To scrouge
1878 To stuff it up
1888 To baste
1888 To belly bump
1888 To score
1889 To bury it
1892 To come about
1893 To flap
1895 To jig-a-jig
1895 To muddle
1895 To nig
1895 To open up
1896 To bumfake

1896 To sew up
1896 To spike
1897 To pestle
1897 To plowter
1897 To quimwedge
1897 To rootle
1897 To roust
1897 To sharge
1897 To smoke
1897 To snabble
1897 To thumb
1897 To toby-tickle
1897 To tump

1900s:

1901 To up
1909 To block
1918 To hop
1921 To love up
1923 To cram
1923 To furgle
1923 To nip
1923 To snizzle
1924 To go all the way
1925 To goose
1925 To rasp
1926 To rock
1927 To cock
1927 To get laid
1928 To jive
1928 To make whoopie
1929 To give it to
1929 To jelly roll

1930 To flop
1946 To party
1946 To shack up with
1951 To pom-pom
1955 To go down
1960 To jag
1961 To jimmy
1961 To pile drive
1966 To honeyfuck
1967 To swing with
1974 To dog
1989 To hound
1997 To breed

2000s:

2001 To jackhammer
2011 To smash out
2012 To pipe

TO ORGASM – VERBS

FEMALE

1300s:

1380 Relieve

1400s:

1450 End
1450 Finish
1450 Release

1500s:

1546 Spend
1574 Bring off
1590 Ecstatic agony
1599 Come

1600s:

1600 Spin off
1618 Come off
1620 Melt
1630 Rapture
1680 Orgasm

1700s:

1743 Spasms
1783 Finale

1800s:

1880 Climax
1888 Pleasure

1900s:

1990 Happy ending

MALE

1400s:

1450 Release

1500s:

1540 Spend
1574 Bring off
1595 Cleave the pin
1599 Come

1600s:

- 1600 Spin off
- 1608 Break his arrow
- 1618 Come off
- 1680 Orgasm

1700s:

- 1743 Spasms
- 1748 Go off
- 1748 Let fly
- 1748 Let go

1800s:

- 1870 Jet his juices
- 1880 Climax
- 1880 Give his gravy
- 1883 Rack someone off
- 1888 Do it
- 1888 Fetch
- 1888 Pleasure
- 1888 Short shoves
- 1888 Spunk
- 1888 Spunking
- 1889 Blow his lump
- 1889 Short digs
- 1890 Shoot his wad

1900s:

- 1905 Get off
- 1915 Cream
- 1915 Shoot his load

1920 Get his gun off
1925 Get them off
1926 Give him a thrill
1926 Thrill
1930 Crack his marbles
1932 Get his nuts off
1932 Get off the button
1935 Ring his bell
1935 Shoot the works
1938 Bust a nut
1938 Nut
1940 Come in his pants
1942 Come
1944 Shoot a wad
1948 Get his rocks off
1950 Get off a nut
1950 Pop a nut
1950 Pop his nuts
1953 Spunk
1956 Make it
1966 Blast off
1966 Blow his socks off
1966 Get his jollies
1966 Jollies
1967 Big O
1969 Pop his cork
1970 Get him off
1971 Blow his wad
1972 Get his balls off
1972 Pop his cookies
1972 Pop his rocks
1974 Bust him out
1975 Shoot his rocks
1978 Pop his wad

1979 Pop his drawers
1990 Happy ending
1995 Break water
1995 Bust water
1998 Get there

2000s:

2000 Bust a shot
2001 Blow his cookies
2001 Blow his juice
2001 Blow his lot
2001 Blow his stack
2002 Spunk off
2002 Spunk up
2003 Blow his tube
2003 Cream the cheese
2003 Get his Jones off

TO EJACULATE – VERBS

1500s:

- 1534 Discharge
- 1590 Piss his tallow

1600s:

- 1626 Shoot
- 1640 Stream
- 1660 Spout
- 1673 Spew

1700s:

- 1704 Fire
- 1748 Inject

1800s:

- 1826 Dub up
- 1837 Shoot

1841 Unload
1850 Fire a shot
1860 Shoot his milt
1879 Shoot his roe
1888 Get off his gun
1890 Squirt his juice
1890 Shoot in the bush
1890 Shoot over the stubble

1900s:

1916 Spoof
1920 Trouser off
1927 Shoot off
1927 Shoot white
1930 Squirt
1943 Shoot the moon
1949 Shoot his bolt
1957 Jazz
1960 Blow his dust
1960 Whitewash
1963 Cream his jeans / pants
1966 Spit
1967 Bullet
1969 Blow his rocks
1969 Chunk out
1970 Blow
1972 Shoot bullets
1972 Snowstorm
1977 Come his fat
1977 Come his lot
1978 Felcher
1980 Shoot his duff
1983 Rinse

1988 Give a facial
1989 Splooge
1989 Spooch
1993 Spuff
1996 Spence
1997 Chuck his muck
1997 Cough his filthy yoghurt
1997 Spooge
1997 Slime
1998 Spreck up
1998 Scum
1999 Face paint
1999 Spaff

2000s:

2000 Bang
2000 Blurt
2000 Bob off
2000 Jam off
2000 Skeet
2000 Spum
2001 Biff
2001 Bust it
2001 Chuck
2003 Baff
2003 Blosh
2003 Bust his meat
2003 Splatter his batter

EXCLAMATIONS!

SURPRISE

600s:

680 Lord!

1100s:

1100 I die!

1200s:

1200 Mercy!

1200 Pray!

1300s:

1330 Pray!

1350 Mary!

1600s:

- 1631 My stars!
- 1672 Agad!
- 1682 Egad!

1700s:

- 1700 What the dogs!
- 1780 Oh, Lor!

1800s:

- 1815 I'll be darned!
- 1829 I'll be blowed!
- 1829 I'm blowed!
- 1838 My sakes!
- 1847 I'll be durned!
- 1897 I'll be goshed!

CURSE!

680s:

- Lord!

1300s:

- 1350 By cock's wounds!
- 1367 By Jesus!
- 1380 By my hood!
- 1386 By cock's bones!

1400s:

- 1465 By cock's body!

1485 By these ten bones!
1499 By cock's blood!

1500s:

1519 Gog's nails!
1533 Gog's body!
1533 By Gog's blood!
1535 Jesus!
1550 By cock!
1562 Blood and nails!
1568 Blood, wounds, and nails!
1573 Nails!
1577 Cods!
1580 By my truly!
1580 Zounds!
1589 Damn it!
1597 Fig me!
1599 Gad's me!

1600s:

1600 Cud's bores!
1600 What the dickens!
1601 By gor!
1604 Cod's life!
1606 Damme!
1607 By gad!
1607 Cuds me!
1607 Damnation!
1616 What a pox!
1653 By cock's death!
1689 By dad!

1700s:

- 1700 Gadzoons!
- 1700 Oh, Crimini!
- 1703 Dash my timbers!
- 1704 Strike me blind!
- 1704 Strike me stupid!
- 1707 Flesh and eels!
- 1709 Thunder!
- 1722 Gosh!
- 1722 Cod!
- 1731 Blood and furies!
- 1735 Blast it!
- 1743 By golly!
- 1748 Blood and thunder!
- 1757 By gosh!
- 1760 Strip me!
- 1766 Strike me ugly!
- 1767 Dad!
- 1772 Strike me stiff!
- 1775 Golly!
- 1780 Laws!
- 1781 Dam!
- 1785 Sakes!
- 1787 Dang!
- 1797 Dash it!
- 1797 Dash me!
- 1799 Gor almighty

1800s:

- 1800 Great guns!
- 1801 Dash my buttons!
- 1805 By gom!
- 1810 Ye stars!

1815 Drat it!
1818 Damn it all!
1819 Blow!
1820 Blow it!
1825 Darnation!
1825 Holy frost!
1830 Cracky!
1831 By gravy!
1832 By Jiminy!
1832 Gosh a-mighty!
1832 Hell's bells!
1832 Oh, crickey!
1834 Christopher!
1835 Dod darn it!
1838 Hell's fire!
1840 Splendiferous!
1845 By jings!
1846 By Joe!
1846 Law sakes!
1847 Great golly!
1847 Snakes alive!
1848 By Jimmy!
1848 Criminy!
1848 Good gad!
1848 Jiminy cricket!
1849 Bust me!
1849 Dash!
1849 For land sakes!
1850 Lawful sakes!
1851 Durn it!
1851 Gee!
1851 Hell's fury!
1856 Geewhitaker!
1856 Gosh dang!

1857 By Godfrey!
1860 Goshdang it!
1861 Shoot!
1862 Sakes alive!
1864 Dammit to hell!
1864 Great Scott!
1866 Crumbs!
1866 Strike me up a tree!
1873 Strike me silly!
1875 Lawsy!
1876 Bust!
1878 Gee whiz!
1879 Great Jehoshaphat!
1880 Muck!
1881 Jumping Jehoshaphat!
1881 Thunder and gimlets!
1883 Gosh darn it!
1883 Judas Priest!
1889 Great snakes!
1897 Christmas!
1897 Holy gee!
1897 Jiminy Christmas!
1898 By jigs!
1899 By Jack!
1899 Good gosh!
1899 Gosh ding!
1899 Holy catfish!
1899 Jigger it!
1899 Strike me perpendicular!

DURING INTERCOURSE

Before 600s:
Ah!

Oh!
Yes!

600s:
680 Lord!

1000s:
1000 I am in heaven!

1100s:
1100 Harder!
1100 I die!
1100 I feel it!
1100 Oh, my heart!
1150 How large it is!

1200s:
1200 Mercy!
1200 Pray!

1300s:
1300 Give me the delicious thing!
1300 How delicious!
1300 Mercy!
1300 Push!
1300 Push me harder!
1300 Push up me!
1300 Push up me as far as you can!
1300 Spare me!

1320 Push me! Push me harder! Push up me!
1330 Pray!
1386 Gadsprecious!

1500s:
1567 Split me!
1580 Shove me! Shove into me!
1593 My stars!
1597 Fig me!

1600s:
1650 It is coming from you!
1682 It gushes inside me!

1700s:
1700 Oh, my!
1720 Do not draw back!
1780 Lor!
1780 Oh, Lor!

1800s:
1838 My sakes!
1840 Splendiferous!
1849 Bust me!
1873 Strike me silly!

APPENDIX A: HISTORICAL SEX SCENE PLANNER

CONTENTS

HISTORICAL SEX SCENE PLANNER: INTRODUCTION

UNDERSTAND THE CONTEXT:

If you have clarity of the period and the context of the moment of intimacy, your sex scene can come across as genuine to the reader. For all of you who enjoy planning your scenes in advance, answer the following questions:

- What year/century and location does this story take place?
- Why does each person love or have a keen interest in the other?
- What is the place/environment? Is it private (i.e., a bedroom)? Is it secretive (i.e., in a closet at a castle ball)? Is it public (i.e., on stage in front of an audience)?
- Who else, if anyone, is in the area? A stranger? A jealous admirer? A secret lover?
- What clothes are they wearing that fit the period?

Knowing the answers to these questions can help prepare you to write your sex scene in a more authentic way.

HISTORICAL SEX SCENE PLANNER: TEMPLATE

UNDERSTAND THE CONTEXT:

What year/century and location does this story take place?

Why does each person love or have a keen interest in the other?

What is the place/environment? Is it private (i.e., a bedroom)? Is it secretive (i.e., in a closet at a castle ball)? Is it public (i.e., on stage in front of an audience)?

Who else, if anyone, is in the area? A stranger? A jealous admirer? A secret lover?

What clothes are they wearing that fit the period?

HISTORICAL SEX SCENE PLANNER: EXAMPLE

Here is an example of how I used the Sex Scene Planner for my naughty novel *Maid Mary and Robin Hood's Merry Men.*

UNDERSTAND THE CONTEXT:

What year/century and location does this story take place?

1500s

Why does each person love or have a keen interest in the other?

Princess Mary loves to take advantage of Badrick the squire's sexual longing for her. Teasing him is fun, boosts her self-esteem, and his handsome features make the game a delight.

Badrick has pure lust over the princess. Game or not, he'll take whatever she'll offer in the way of pleasure.

What is the place/environment? Is it private (i.e., a bedroom)? Is it secretive (i.e., in a closet at a castle ball)? Is it public (i.e., on stage in front of an audience)?

Princess Mary's chilly chamber in the king's castle at night.

Who else, if anyone, is in the area? A stranger? A jealous admirer? A secret lover?

Maid Dinah is helping princess Mary undress for the evening.

What clothes are they wearing that fit the period?

Princess Dinah: A red corset over a long, white chemise
Badrick: A tunic, brown coat, and brown trousers
Maid Dinah: A moss green dress

Knowing the answers to these questions, I now know what nouns I can use for the period, why the couple would enjoy the interaction, how the setting might fit the circumstance, who else could be a party to the intimate moment, and how the clothes might play a role in the act.

Dinah paused at working the corset's laces, then sighed. "Your young lover is snooping again."

"What lover?" There was no man intimate in her life.

Dinah nodded to the ajar bedroom door.

Mary smiled at the handsome squire, Badrick, peeking through the opening.

"Let's have some fun, Dinah," Mary whispered, then called

out, "Oh, Badrick. Your timing is well. Would you assist Maid Dinah?"

With a sheepish grin of being caught, he stepped through the doorway. "Your Highness?"

Badrick's hair was still as scruffy as when he was a boy and they flirted on the steep hills behind the castle, but now his high cheekbones were sharper. His lips fuller. The perfect invitation for kissing. And his eyes? Gorgeous. They were a topaz more precious and innocent than years ago.

"Come here, boy." Mary made sure her tone was kind and inviting, not angry.

He shuffled a bit further into the room.

Mary laughed. "Closer."

His steps still kept him at a distance.

"Closer," she sang.

He approached to be arm's length from her. She tapped the tight cloth wrapped around her waist.

"It is called a 'corset,'" she said. "Do you think it will become the new fashion?"

He shrugged.

"I believe it will," Mary said. "I must take it off now. I need you to hold it as Dinah unlaces it in the back."

He paused, nodded, and stepped forward.

Badrick surveyed her chest trying to figure out where to grip the corset. She held back the giggles that wanted to burst out. How darling he was.

He settled on holding the top lining that sloped under her armpits. Her giggle burst forth.

"Not there, silly. I'm too ticklish there." She guided his soft hands to the firm material that covered her nipples. "Hold it here."

But he held the edge of the material between his thumb and forefinger as if he were holding fragile teacups.

"Don't be gentle, Badrick. The corset mustn't fall. That

would be indecent." She planted her hands over his, mashing his hands against her breasts. He gasped. "Excellent. Keep your hands there as Dinah finishes unlacing it."

Mary didn't let go of the squire's strong hands. Instead, she pressed his hands firm against her breasts. It was adorable how his eyes widened, dancing back and forth between her breasts and her face. Dinah had the good sense to play along by working at a snail's pace.

"Badrick," Mary said. "Remember when we were children and played hide and seek in the hills?"

"Y-yes, Your Highness."

"Often, I reflect on the early mornings when we played there, how wet the dew was, as though the good Lord poured cream all over them. I think of those creamy mounds and cup those fond memories close to my beating heart."

She squeezed his hands to her chest, so he could feel her hardening nipples in his palms. The tingling at her breasts warmed her chest, a nice solution to the chilly room.

"Do you remember, Badrick?" She shook his hands, her breasts jiggling in his grasp.

He gulped and stammered, "Yes, Your Highness."

"Sometimes, when the day was hot and I was absolutely fatigued, climbing felt quite long and hard," Mary said. "But I pushed myself and still climbed up them."

His eyes fixed on hers and his jaw dropped.

She clutched his hands to her breasts with every repeating word. "I pushed and pushed. Pushed and pushed. Becoming hotter and hotter. Higher and higher and higher. I remember it so well, those wonderful memories growing inside me. Growing and growing. Filling me and filling me. I can practically feel myself there. I feel myself, feel myself, feel myself there now."

His hands twitched, making slight groping motions. Poor

boy. He must have been fighting the temptation to clamp her breasts in his fists.

"Do you feel it, too, Badrick?" Shaking his firm hands, she jiggled her breasts in his grip once more. "Do you feel those creamy hills, how hot and long and hard it sometimes was to climb them?"

He could only nod. What a handsome shade of red his face became!

"Do those lovely memories fill you with pleasure the way they penetrate me, and fill me inside with gushing delight?"

He opened his mouth to speak but nothing came out. His hands clenched her breasts sending a nice prickling sensation to her core.

"Done, milady," Dinah said.

Alas. The delightful game was over.

"Very good. Thank you, Dinah." Mary released her hold of Badrick's hands and clasped the sides of the corset. But the boy kept his hands pressed to her breasts. She smirked. "You may let go, now, Badrick."

"Yes, Your Highness. My apologies." He dropped his hands to his side.

"Here you are, Dinah." Mary handed the corset to her.

Dinah stepped away to set the corset down. Hands free, Mary caressed through her chemise her happy breasts.

"How good it is to be free from such confines. The corset rubs hard against my breasts."

Her stiff nipples poked out through the fabric. The boy, still standing a mere breath away, couldn't pull his gaze from her touching herself.

She smirked. "They've gotten bigger, haven't they, Badrick?"

At last, his stare returned to her face. "Your Highness?"

"My breasts. Back when we were babes and bathed

together, I didn't have these, did I? Don't they look bigger to you?"

He glanced between her bosom and her face, as if unsure what was proper. "Uh..."

"By the looks of it, you've grown, too." She nodded to his tenting crotch, imagining how large his prick was under his trousers. She patted him down there. "Perhaps you should go to your bed and take care of yourself."

"Yes, Your Highness." He adjusted himself and waddled out the door.

Convinced he was out of earshot, Mary let her laughter fly. Dinah joined in.

"Did you see his face?" Mary squeaked.

Dinah managed to say through guffaws. "I was too focused on his prick downstairs, concerned he'd wet his pants."

APPENDIX B: A TIP, JUST THE TIP - USING HISTORICAL SYNONYMS

APPENDIX B: A TIP, JUST THE TIP - USING HISTORICAL SYNONYMS

By replacing modern nouns with historical nouns, the writing can sound more authentic to your story's historical setting. However, mentioning too many genitals can sound absurd, so I like to try limiting how often I mention them.

For example, suppose we take a 1600s sex scene that uses modern language.

She lay on the hay naked in the cold outdoors, her heart thumping as she looked upon his own naked form. He was gazing at her, a hungry grin on his lips, his arms at his side.

Holy shit! He already had a hard-on, and it was huge! She nearly gushed just thinking of him entering her with that large dick.

He crawled on top of her and kissed her. His lips tasted sweet. She opened her legs to invite him in, but he moved down to her breasts.

"Damn! You've got such a beautiful rack! I gotta have a taste."

He licked her nipples, swirling his tongue around each one until they were glistening in the moonlight.

He then kissed her again and eased his manhood into her.

Holy moly! His wonderful member popped all sorts of excitement across her skin.

"Oh my god!" he said. "Your pussy feels amazing!"

He jack-hammered in and out of her. Throughout several minutes of his pumping her, she shuddered a few times. After her fourth orgasm, he grunted.

"I'm going to come," he said.

Uh, oh. She didn't want to get pregnant. But she didn't want to ruin his orgasm, either.

"Fuck me in the ass," she said.

He paused and looked at her. Apparently understanding her intentions, he pulled out of her and she got on her hands and knees.

He grabbed her butt cheeks and spread her open. He guided his cock to her asshole and prodded around, seeking her entrance.

She reached underneath and rubbed her clit. Yes! That felt wonderful!

He squeezed into her dark channel, and it was only a matter of a few thrusts before he came inside.

She fingered her clit to one more climax, then he gently lay upon her, and they slid flat upon the hay, his cock still buried in her bowels.

It was lovely feeling his heavy body on top of her, comforting even. Soon he softened and slipped out of her. He rolled off and turned her to lie with her face-to-face, and she fell asleep in his arms.

Now to replace some of the modern terms with ones more relevant to the times of the 1600s.

She lay on the hay naked in the cold outdoors, her heart thumping as she looked upon his own naked form. He was gazing at her, a hungry grin on his lips, his arms at his side.

Mercy! He already had a stiff stander, and it was huge! She nearly gushed merely thinking of him entering her with that large staff.

He crawled on top of her and kissed her. His lips tasted sweet. She opened her legs to invite him in, but he moved down to her breasts.

"Fig me! You've got such beautiful heavers! I must have a taste."

He licked her nipples, swirling his tongue around each one until they were glistening in the moonlight.

He then kissed her again and eased his prick into her.

My stars! His wonderful rod popped all sorts of excitement across her skin.

"By cock's bones!" he said. "Your twat feels amazing!"

He niggled in and out of her. Throughout several minutes of his grinding her, she shuddered a few times. After her fourth spend, he grunted.

"I'm going to come," he said.

Uh, oh. She didn't wish to get pregnant. But she didn't want to ruin his spend, either.

"Fuck me in the arse," she said.

He paused and regarded her. Apparently understanding her intentions, he uprooted himself from her and she shifted to her hands and knees.

He grabbed her cheeks and spread her open. He guided

his cock to her nockhole and prodded around, seeking her entrance.

She reached underneath and rubbed her clit. Yes! That felt wonderful!

He squeezed into her back gate, and it was only a matter of a few strokes before he came inside.

She frigged her clit to one more spend, then he gently lay upon her, and they slid flat upon the hay, his cock still buried in her arse.

It was lovely feeling his heavy body on top of her, comforting even. Soon he softened and slipped out of her. He rolled off and turned her to lie with her face-to-face, and she fell asleep in his arms.

Not perfect, but better. And that's what we're going for.

Let's do another, this time using an approach that avoids mentioning as many body parts as possible. The goal is to avoid sounding like a doctor giving a lecture. We'll replace the clinical words for genitalia with suggestive, emotional words while avoiding laughable euphemisms.

She lay on the hay naked in the cold outdoors, her heart thumping as she looked upon his own naked form. He was gazing at her, a hungry grin on his lips, his arms at his side.

Mercy! He was already stiff, and he was huge! Merely thinking of him entering her got her wet.

He crawled on top of her and kissed her. His lips tasted sweet. She opened her legs to invite him in, but he moved down to her breasts.

"Fig me! Your look delicious! I must have a taste."

He licked her nipples, swirling his tongue around each one until they were glistening in the moonlight.

He then kissed her again and eased himself into her.

My stars! His entrance set free all sorts of excitement across her skin.

"By cock's bones!" he said. "You feel amazing!"

They undulated together. She shuddered with spasms a few times. After her fourth, he grunted.

"I'm going to come," he said.

Uh, oh. She didn't wish to get pregnant. But she didn't want to ruin his spend, either.

"Enter me another way," she said.

He paused and regarded her. Apparently understanding her intentions, he uprooted himself from her and she shifted to her hands and knees.

His desire guided him and he inched into her dark passage.

She reached underneath and rubbed herself. Yes! That felt wonderful!

He squeezed deep within her, and it was only a matter of a few strokes before he achieved his release.

She managed one more spend, then he gently lay upon her, and they slid flat upon the hay. He remained lodged inside her.

It was lovely feeling his heavy body on top of her, comforting even. Soon he softened and slipped out of her. He rolled off and turned her to lie with her face-to-face, and she fell asleep in his arms.

Lastly, let's add archaic-sounding phrasing. Tricky, because doing so can yank the reader out of the story. This is one of those cases when yanking is not a good thing. Better to use this method of archaic-sounding syntax sparingly.

She lay naked on the hay in the cold outdoors. Her heart thumped when she set her eyes upon his naked form. His arms remained at his side and his gaze matched his hungry grin.

Mercy! Already was he stiff and huge! Merely the thought of him entering her soaked her.

He crawled on top of her and kissed her. His lips tasted of fine mead. She opened her legs to invite him in, but he moved down to her breasts.

"Fig me! Your look delicious! I must have a taste."

He licked her nipples, swirling his tongue around each until they glistened in the moonlight.

He then kissed her again and eased himself into her.

My stars! His entrance set free a plentitude of excitement across her skin.

"By cock's bones!" he said. "You feel amazing!"

They undulated together. Intermittently did she shudder with spasms. After her fourth, he grunted.

"I shall soon come," he said.

Uh, oh. She had no wish to become pregnant. But neither had she the desire to ruin his spend.

"Enter me in another fashion," she said.

He paused and regarded her. With apparent understanding of her intentions, he uprooted himself from her and she shifted to her hands and knees.

His desire guided him and he inched into her dark passage.

She reached underneath and rubbed herself. Yes! How wonderful that felt!

He squeezed deep within her and, in a few strokes, he achieved his release.

She managed one more spend, then he gently lay upon her, and they slid flat upon the hay. He remained lodged inside her.

How lovely was the feeling of his heavy body atop of her. Comforting even. Soon did he soften and slip out of her. He rolled off and repositioned her to lie with her face-to-face, and she fell asleep in his arms.

I wrote a series of short stories using that last method of phrasing called *De Sade and Grimm.* The stories take place in Medieval England and involve a female warrior fighting sadistic paranormal beasts. While some readers loved the archaic-sounding phrasing, others despised it because the phrasing was hard to read, required a little extra work to comprehend, and took them out of the story. As a result, in the book store's descriptions of the stories, I included a warning of the archaic-sounding syntax and gave an example. That way, only readers who were able to enjoy the example would buy the stories.

Which method appeals to you most? What might you add or change? Play with it!

APPENDIX C: FIND AND REPLACE

APPENDIX C: FIND AND REPLACE

To make my Middle Ages fiction sound more historical, I created this list of words to do a "Find and Replace" search.

Words to replace in no particular order:

Got to, have to ➡ must

So, ➡ thus,

Okay ➡ As you will, that is well, very well

I think ➡ No doubt

Fine. (Eye roll) ➡ Oh by Gog, I surrender, as you will

No! ➡ I dare not, I must not, by no means

Over there ➡ Yonder

Have at it ➡ Do as you will

Mental: what bothers you, what's the problem, what's the matter? ➡ what troubles you, pains you?

Physical: what bothers you, what's the matter? ➡ what ails you, what agitates you so?

Pretty (as in, pretty good, pretty painful) ➡ rather

A young woman ➡ wench

A young virtuous woman ➡ maid, maiden

Stop, wait ➡ stay

What do you mean? ➡ What is it you ask?

I didn't [verb] [noun] ➞ I [verb] no [noun]

I promise ➞ by my troth, I vow

Actually ➞ in truth, in faith, verily, rather, indeed, truly

Thank you ➞ I thank thee, my gratitude, I am in your debt, my gratitude to you, you are most kind, you are most gracious

Hi, Hello ➞ Well met! What ho!

How are you? ➞ How fare thee?

Want ➞ wish

Go ahead ➞ carry on, keep on

Good morning ➞ Good morrow!

Good afternoon ➞ Good morrow!

Please, ➞ Pray thee, by all means, if you please, I beg of thee

Tell me, ➞ Pray tell,

Goodbye, bye, farewell ➞ Fare thee well, farewell

Oh, well ➞ so be it, no matter

Excuse me ➞ I beg your pardon, pray pardon me

I'm going to ➞ mean to, plan to, aim to

Never mind ➞ Pay no heed

Sorry (apology) ➞ Alas, pray pardon me

This time ➞ Now

That is, I mean ➞ indeed, verily, rather, such is

Maybe ➞ perhaps, perchance

I'm happy, thankful, glad ➞ it pleases me

I'm fine ➞ I'm of good health

Just ➞ merely

Besides, ➞ after all,

God! ➞ Have mercy! Lord!

I don't know ➞ I know not, I know scarcely what (s)he...

I don't understand ➞ I know scarcely what you are suggesting, I am puzzled, I am mystified, I am perplexed, I know not what you mean

Curse you, damn you ➡ Fie upon thee! A plague upon thee!

Darn it! ➡ Dash it!

Not true! Impossible! ➡ Fiddlesticks!

Wow! Unbelievable! ➡ Zounds! By God's wounds!

Or else ➡ lest

Do me a favor ➡ do me a kindness

Room ➡ chambers

Do your (chores), do my (tasks) ➡ attend to (your, my, her, his)

Don't (whine) ➡ Spare me (your patter)

Shut up ➡ Spare me

Yes ➡ yea, yes

APPENDIX D: LIZ'S FAVORITES - NOUNS

APPENDIX D: LIZ'S FAVORITES - NOUNS

Nouns

Breasts:

Apples

Nipples:

Cherries

Clit:

Clit
Clitoris
Nub
Bud
Button
Pearl

Pubic Hair:

Fur
Bush
Thicket
Tuft

Thicket
Down

Vagina (From early to late):
Quaint
Trench
Altar of Venus
Cunny
Quiver
Womb
Engine
Entrance
Garden
Lips
Muff
Pussy
Sheath
Slit
Burrow
Charms
Cleft
Gash
Kitty
Quim
Sex
Snatch
Cauldron
Cave
Chasm
Crevice
Down below
Heaven
Tunnel
Pussycat

Penis (From early to late):
Cock
Column
Spigot
Staff
Prick
Rod
Lance
Ramrod
Shaft
Throbbing mass
Truncheon
Bludgeon
Bayonet
Dick
Instrument
Manhood
Member
Musket
Tool
Length
Muscle

Testicles:
Balls
Nuts
Nutsack
Pair
Sack

Ass:
Arse
Behind

Backside
Buttocks
Cheeks
Rear
Bottom
Buns
Butt
Tush

Rectum:
Anus
Backdoor
Orifice
Back avenue
Channel
Crevice
Rectum
Asshole
Back entrance
Butthole
Tail
Back alley

Semen:
Butter
Marrow
Cream
Milk
Roe
Emissions
Fluid
Discharge
Jism
Seed

Semen
Spunk
Tallow
Cum
Goo
Load
Spooge
Wad

Vaginal Discharge:
Cream
Emissions
Juice
Cooze
Cum

YOUR PERSONAL FAVORITES

Note down here which nouns are your favorites so that you don't need to keep flipping through the pages.

AUTHOR'S NOTE

I hope this has been, and will often be, a helpful resource for you.

Having written so much erotica (20 books and counting!), I thought this *Thesaurus for Romance Writers* series would be a great venue to drip some of my favorite writing techniques. And I hope that by the end, I wasn't the only one dripping.

Please let me know if there are sections and terms you uncovered that are missing from these books so that I may update them. You can email me at LizAdams-Books@gmail.com and put THESAURUS WORDS in all-caps in the subject line so that I don't accidentally miss your email.

Also, check out the other books in this series if you want more synonym help: *Arousing Adjectives* and *Voluptuous Verbs*.

And hey! I encourage you to try all the exercises and templates in this series. Every master starts a disaster. The way to master your writing is by drafting and editing and getting feedback on your writing, over and over.

The good news is that writing sex scenes is fun!

As my friend and author Chloe Adler once said in describing the process of writing erotica, "You write some, then go to bed. Write some more, then go to bed. Write some more, then go to bed." Your readers will get the benefit of reading your steamy scenes in bed without having to alternate.

For all you readers of saucy tales, if you're interested in discovering which sexy superhero you are, take my quiz at http://www.LizAdamsAuthor.com. You can also join my reader community and get a free short story about what Wonder Woman's sex life might be like!

UNLOCK THE SECRETS TO WRITING IRRESISTIBLE SEX SCENES

Discover the Perfect Words to Elevate Your Romantic Scenes

This *Thesaurus for Romance Writers* series comprises of three passionate volumes dripping to satisfy your needs, each designed to elevate your writing and make your love scenes steamy:

1. Voluptuous Verbs

Why settle for mundane descriptions like "she took off his pants" when you can spice things up. Replace it with, "She unbuckled, unzipped, and unsteadied him." Find verbs that penetrate your scenes and leave your readers panting. This thesaurus includes writing tips on how to use the bedroom scene to develop the heroine's inner growth, her inner and outer consequences, the relationship's consequences, the subtext of the scene, and the wild card.

2. Arousing Adjectives

While overusing adjectives in regular scenes is a faux pas, they are indispensable when the clothes come off and the lovemaking begins. Dive into words that paint vivid pictures, like "sprouting, thick, eager, hot, frenzied, throbbing, strong," for him, and "supple, taut, pluckable, quivering, tangy, velvety, wet," for her. These adjectives will transform your spicy scenes into scenes your readers will read again and again. Included in this thesaurus are exercise on how to write at different heat levels, and how to incorporate the character's goal, motivation, conflict, and stakes in your delectable, lip-smacking scenes.

3. Naughty Nouns (this book)

A perfect resource for historical romance writers! This book of synonyms is your go-to guide to determine whether grabbing hold of his "length" fits the time period of your Regency romance. Which terms did they use back then? Discover the historically accurate terms that set the mood just right. This thesaurus includes tips on how to use explicit words to incite excitement instead of sounding like an anatomical textbook.

A Must-Have Resource for Every Romance Writer

Whether you're crafting a steamy Regency romance or a contemporary love story, use the books in the *Thesaurus for Romance Writers* series — invaluable resources that will help you find the perfect words to set hearts racing and pulses pounding in your spicy scenes with captivating synonyms. It has been a game-changer for me, and I hope it will be for you too.

ACKNOWLEDGMENTS

I started the *Thesaurus for Romance Writers* series when historical author and friend Regina Kammer guided me and other authors to Jonathon Green's outstanding online interactive timeline of sexy terms and their first moments of popular use (thetimelinesofslang.com). The timeline focused on historical synonyms for genitalia and intercourse.

From there, I launched into other sources, ones which provided synonyms for words not addressed by Green's timeline. Websites such as Etymonline the Online Etymology Dictionary (etymonline.com), The Historical Thesaurus of English (historicalthesaurus.arts.gla.ac.uk) and Google's etymology when searching definitions.

Over the years of dedicated thesaurus usage, the list of words became longer. And, oh, much longer. After reading such historical erotica like *The Autobiography of a Flea* and *My Secret Life: An Erotic Diary of Victorian London,* and after finding a few short lists of sensual terms elsewhere, I added even more words to the mix.

Once I completed the list, I studied the layouts of other romance-oriented thesaurus books—including ones by Cara Bristol, Valerie Howard, and Stefanie Olsen—and determined the layout I thought was most useful.

Lastly, my brilliant writing coach Beth Barany helped me with edits and ways to market this series.

The inviting covers were designed by 100 Covers, and I appreciate all the hard work they put into the design.

And thank you, dear writer. The world needs your stories. *I* need your stories.

Keep writing!

~Liz

ABOUT THE AUTHOR

Award-winning author of best-selling spicy, paranormal fairytales, Liz Adams tires her hands at the keyboard spinning steamy, surrealistic fantasies — some historical, some contemporary, some futuristic — so that her readers can also tire out their hands until the happy endings. She loves leaving her readers breathless and soaked.

Want to know a secret? Playing loud music while reading might hide your squeals of delight. Just sayin'.

She lives in the gorgeous San Francisco Bay Area, and in her spare time, she enjoys movies on the couch cuddling with her spouse and two cats.

If you enjoyed this book, please write a review!

Liz would love to know how you heard about her ebook, so drop her a line at LizAdamsBooks@gmail.com or at her website:

http://www.LizAdamsAuthor.com.

She's always eager to connect with her readers and would love to hear from you.

MORE BOOKS BY WRITER'S FUN ZONE PUBLISHING

Overcome Writer's Block: A Self-Guided Creative Writing Class to Get You Writing Again

(Writer's Fun Zone Book 1)

The Writer's Adventure Guide: 12 Stages to Writing Your Book for Novelists and Creative Nonfiction Writers

(Writer's Fun Zone Book 2)

Twitter for Authors: Social Media Book Marketing Strategies for Shy Writers

(Writer's Fun Zone Book 3)

Plan Your Novel Like a Pro: And Have Fun Doing It!

(Writer's Fun Zone Book 4)

7 Essential Keys to Planning Your Novel: Story Preparation for Pantsers

(Writer's Fun Zone Book 5)

Mastering Deep Point of View: Simple Steps to Make Your Stories Irresistible to Your Readers

by Alice Gaines

ALSO BY LIZ ADAMS

FAIRY TALE EROTICA

ALICE'S SALACIOUS ADVENTURES, LESSONS FROM WONDERLAND

(Adventures of Alice, Book 1)

A titillating two-book collection

ALICE'S STORY OF O, PRINCESS AND THE PEA

(Adventures of Alice, Book 2)

An interactive, spicy fairytale

ALICE'S FRISKY FREAKY FRIDAY, HANSEL AND GRETEL

(Adventures of Alice, Book 3)

A body-swapping, dark fairytale

ALICE'S SNOW WHITE AND THE SEVEN SINS

(Adventures of Alice, Book 4)

A reverse-harem spicy fairytale

ALICE'S LABOR OF LOVE, TASTING CINDERELLA

(Adventures of Alice, Book 5)

An intoxicating, oral fairytale

ALICE'S STUDY IN LITTLE DEATHS, AESOP'S FABLES

(Adventures of Alice, Standalone)

A suspenseful, spicy fairytale

GOLDIE'S LOCKS AND THE THREE MEN

(A Modern Erotic Fairy Tale Fantasy for Women)

What if the only way to find the right man was to instead find the right men?

Ariel's Super Power of Love

Ever wonder what Wonder Woman's love life was like?

Sherlock; The Casebook of a Salacious Sleuth

(4 Spicy Romantic Short Stories)

Feeding his carnal appetite one case at a time.

de Sade & Grimm; A Spicy Collection of Dark Delights

(4 Supernatural Short Stories)

Can you resist the pleasure when evil claims you?

The Origin of Tinkerbell

(A Modern Erotic Fairy Tale Fantasy for Women)

Time stops for the playful.

Maid Mary and Robin Hood's Merry Men

(A Dark Romance)

A mask can hide you from yourself.

What if your beloved paralyzed you and removed your mask?

SHORT STORIES

Amy "Red" Riding's Hood

(Fairy Tale Erotica)

Would you submit to the beast within him?

Breaking Free

(A Kidnapping Romance)

When society suppresses your femininity and your kidnapper encourages it, how can you hate him?

Alina Said, Call Me Maybe

(A Short Romance)

How far would you go, letting a stranger caress you in public?

Sherlock; The Case of the Ripped Bodice

(A Spicy Romantic Short Story #1)

Your client fears he may be Jack the Ripper? Terrific.

Sherlock; The Case of the Invisible Lover

(A Spicy Romantic Short Story #2)

Who haunts her bed?

Sherlock; The Case of Sinbad's Seduction

(A Spicy Romantic Short Story #3)

What will you do when a night of vengeful passion leads to a perilous mystery?

Sherlock; The Case of the Voyeuristic Vampire

(A Spicy Romantic Short Story #4)

His penetrating gaze awakens your desires.

de Sade and Grimm; An Enchantment of Leaves

(A Dark Supernatural Short Story #1)

What if an unholy fiend unleashed your darkest desires?

de Sade and Grimm; A Seduction of Clay

(A Dark Supernatural Short Story #2)

You awake. No memory. The Clay Master claims he is your husband. Will you yield?

de Sade and Grimm; An Ambush of Cream

(A Dark Supernatural Short Story #3)

How can she fight the invisible, hedonistic foe?

de Sade and Grimm; A Menace of Silk

(A Dark Supernatural Short Story #4)

What invisible force is hell-bent on claiming her?

SHORT STORIES IN ANTHOLOGIES

"The Artist" in Sensexual: A Unique Anthology 2013 Vol 1

If you were a succubus and spotted his morning growth, what would you do?